SIX-GUN SHOWDOWN

Nobody noticed the batwings being brushed open until the man who entered said, "Been a long haul, Teddy."

"Bonner Hudson?" Somehow the Kid kept from firing when he realized Bonner hadn't drawn his six-gun. He looked around, and it seemed everyone in the saloon was rooted to their chairs. Enjoying the sudden limelight, and keeping his eyes glued on Bonner, he announced: "Just passing through your town. Name's Kid LaDuke. And this hombre calls himself a tracker."

"Is she still alive?" Bonner asked calmly.

"You any good with that hogiron, Mr. Hudson?"

This was going to end in bloodshed, Bonner knew; Teddy LaDuke wasn't about to give up his guns. "Folks, I'm packing a badge. This man kidnapped my daughter. He's got a lot of blood on his hands." Then, "Yup, LaDuke, I'll oblige you."

"Then you'll never find out what happened to her, Bonner, 'cause you'll be dead!"

ROBERT KAMMEN

THE GUNS OF KID LaDUKE

ZEBRA BOOKS
KENSINGTON PUBLISHING CORP.

ZEBRA BOOKS

are published by

Kensington Publishing Corp.
475 Park Avenue South
New York, NY 10016

First Printing: April, 1993

Printed in the United States of America

Prologue

Kid LaDuke was reported to have been the prettiest baby ever born in the Flathead Valley. Even today a daguerreotype hangs in Albert's Photo Shop over at Pablo taken when the Kid was scarcely a year old. Scrawled in one corner is his given name, Lawrence Teddy LaDuke. You add color to the picture and you'd have a blush on the high cheekbones and a touch of blue livening up the soulful eyes. Framing the cherubic face was curly black hair still uncut so that it caressed the Kid's shoulders. The smile was bubbly as sassafras fizzing on a hot summer day.

Along about his seventeenth birthday the Kid and some of his chums got on their ponies and headed over to Lone Tree. They pulled in as planned after sundown, but held out along the Little Bitterroot River while one of them went into town to procure whiskey from the Crooked Spike saloon. Then they settled in to wait until the single downtown street was quiet.

When a half moon passed behind the snowy brow

of Snowshoe Peak, four empty whiskey bottles splashed into the river to bob away. Along with the Kid there were six others letting their horses walk out from under the aspens. Lone Tree didn't have many commercial enterprises other than the Crooked Spike, Skinner's trading post, and an assay office run by a man who cut hair on the side. Money hadn't brought the Kid here, but guns had, as here in Lone Tree a master gunsmith plied his trade. They didn't even have to break in to Clive Brewster's place; one of the Kid's chums had a key that would unlock the gunsmith's front door.

As they came onto the barren street, passing between the few business places closed down for the night, a dog came snarling out, and the Kid snapped, "Orville, take care of that mutt." The others drew rein behind the Kid as Orville Newton whistled softly to draw the dog over.

Newton didn't have a gun, but he had a pigsticker of a knife, which he pulled out of his beltline as he slid down from his horse. "You remember me . . . yeah, boy . . . ease over here now." The dog began whining as it padded up to Newton, and then it hopped up to set its front paws on his chest as he stroked its shaggy back and head. The stroke changed to a hard gripping of his hand clamping the jaws shut as he brought the knife blade slicing across the mongrel's throat. He flung the dog away to keep blood from spurting onto his trousers. "Just like stickin' a pig," he chortled.

"Shut the hell up, Orville. There's light still showin' at the gunsmith's. Damn."

"He do work late at times."

"We gonna pull back?"

Kid LaDuke pondered this as the others came in closer. Where before they had been uncertain about coming over here, the Kid could see in their eyes that they were whiskey brave. Like Newton, some of them didn't have guns but only knives, and to start a life of crime, as they'd vowed back at Pablo, a gunhand needed the accoutrements a gunsmith could supply. Another thought bantered about on the way over here concerned those two daughters of Clive Brewster's. The family had quarters above the gunshop. The gang noticed dark windows on the upper floor of the gunshop at the end of the street. Decked out in a cast-off gray flannel shirt, Levi's snucked down over un-spurred boots that were run down at the heels, and a Stetson he'd spent considerable time nursing into shape, the Kid bubbled out a grin.

"What the hell, we're here . . . and we need guns. Hand over that key. Jimmy, you go with Orville, and then let Orville knock on the back door. Tell Brewster you just dropped by, but the Crooked Spike was closed . . . thought you'd just drop by since you seen he was still working. Can you remember that? Just don't be flashin' no weapons."

The other chums of the Kid's went with him to tie up their horses as quiet as they could, though one of the horses got to whickering. With the key in hand, but not bothering to unlimber the old single-action Navy Colt, the Kid glided up to open the screen door, as clustering in close, the four others, their eyes shining in the light of the half moon, tried not to show

7

their nervousness. The key made a rasping noise in the lock, but the Kid managed to unlock the door and bring it ajar on oiled hinges. He could hear Orville's high-pitched voice coming from the gun shop, and then the Kid and his youthful cohorts were slipping in.

The back of the shop, where Brewster did his work, was separated from the front area by a short hallway. The doors at either end of the hallway stood open, and a flight of stairs began midway up the hallway.

Someone with the Kid had the misfortune to bump something off a glass display case. Back in the gunshop the gunsmith heard something hitting the floor. Glimpsing Orville Newton, he realized what this was all about. Desperately he tried reaching for a Colt's Peacemaker an arm's length away on his workbench, and it wasn't a dog Orville used his knife on this time, but a man. The blade of his knife went in deep, bringing a look of shocked disbelief to the gunsmith's face, as well as to Orville Newton's. He'd never killed a man before, neither had any of the others, and as the gunsmith folded down at his feet, it was Jimmy, another fifteen-year-old, who blurted out, "The Kid said this might happen." Orville Newton looked up from the body sprawled on the floor at Kid LaDuke appearing behind his drawn six-gun.

"You damn fool," LaDuke hissed, "shut the back door."

"I, Kid . . . he's dead. . . ."

"Quit your blubbering, Orville, and fetch that light up here." There was in the Kid's blue eyes a strange glitter, more than the excitement of the moment, and not a trace of the nervousness the others were sharing.

When the Kid had come down the hallway, he'd sent two others up the staircase after Brewster's daughters. Somehow he resented that it had been Orville killing the gunsmith and not him. He motioned for Orville to set the coal oil lamp on one of the display cases, and to draw the heavy window shades. In cases nailed to the walls were an assortment of rifles. The floor display cases contained a lot of handguns, and the Kid and the others lost little time in picking out what each considered a favorite brand. They also found, in wall cabinets and in lower-case drawers, supple leather holsters and gunbelts and boxes of shells. It was a bonanza of weaponry that got the Kid to wishing they'd brought along a packhorse.

"Here," the Kid snickered, "you'll need one of these scabbards for that Winchester. You others, settle down now as people live hereabouts."

"Hey, what's this?"

"Trot that whiskey out," another snorted with an eager smile. "How do I look?"

"You put another gunbelt across your chest, Jimmy, and the first river we cross you'll drown. Take off that stuff and ease out front. Everything's quiet, bring back our saddlebags."

As Jimmy was slipping back into the gunshop, a muffled scream fled down the staircase. The soft chatter cut away as everyone exchanged glances, in their eyes now an anticipatory lust. More than once they'd seen the nubile daughters of the gunsmith parading around Lone Tree. Most of them had never been with a woman before, and it was this mystery coupled with all the whiskey in their bellies that brought them toward the hallway. Only the Kid thought to bring along the lamp. Even the Kid had forgotten that two horses tethered out back and five more out in the street would attract a curious eye, but one thing Lone Tree didn't have was a lawman.

The passage of a couple of hours had seen the Brewster girls ravaged many times where they lay tied to their four-posters in separate upstairs bedrooms. The Kid was the last to leave with Orville Newton's pigsticker in hand as the others trooped in various stages of disarray down the staircase. Mercifully both girls had passed out, and the Kid found it easier to kill them. He came downstairs on unconcerned feet, and before long they were heading out of Lone Tree, not back to Pablo but to head through mountain passes to the haven of other high valleys.

Later on he would say that Orville Newton had killed the gunsmith's daughters, but by then Orville and the Kid's other chums would be dead. By then Kid LaDuke would be somewhat older, wearing a notched Colt's Peacemaker and heading up a gang of desperados. And you know, that picture of the Kid's was still on display over at Pablo. Along with a fresh Wanted every now and then showing that same old bubbly smile.

Chapter One

When Kid LaDuke left the Flathead Valley he flung out a vow he'd never return. And the Kid hadn't ever since those killings at Lone Tree. The Kid's misadventures had taken him down into lower Idaho and Nevada. One by one his old chums had gone down, while the Kid hadn't even been scratched in a number of deadly gun battles. The fact he seemed to lead a charmed life was a magnet for high riders anxious to join the Kid's gang.

Less than two years later, the summer of '79 when Kid LaDuke reached his nineteenth birthday, an article in a Nevada newspaper was brought to his attention. The gang had just been chased out of Utah into Nevada in possession of a lot of Mormon greenbacks, but at a cost, as two that rode with the Kid had been captured. That hadn't kept them from seeking Owyhee as a good place to hole up, along with a vicious rainstorm that was threatening to wash boardwalks and a goodly portion of the town into the river of the same name.

"Dancy Stuart—now what kind of sissy name is that."

11

"I only wish I had Dancy's money," retorted Kid LaDuke as he swilled the beer around in his glass. "Bought himself quite a racehoss."

"See, Kid, that damned hoss is worth twenty-five thousand dollars. That's more'n we got from those black-hearted Mormons. Says here too, Kid, he owns the top dog ranch up where you was reared."

"I can read, Wiley. So, he bought hisself a hoss. If I had half his money I'd invest in a chain of whorehouses."

Tipping his hat back from where he sat across the table in the Owyhee bar taken over by the hardcases, Inky Braxton said, "Seems to me, Kid, you was talkin' about goin' back there. This is as good an excuse as any to go."

"Lean in while I tell you why I haven't gone back." The Kid refilled his glass from a pitcher. "As you know I'm a damned good tracker."

"Hell, Kid, you're the best I've ever seen. One reason we've kept ahead of John Law."

"There's one better." A smile shone through the stubble on Kid LaDuke's cherubic face. He'd filled out more, had a jaunty cut to his trailworn clothing, and there was a matching Colt's Peacemaker snuggled at his left hip. He wore black leather wristbands and a black silky bandanna. "He took me under his wing, otherwise I wouldn't be here enjoying such pleasant company."

"I expect this'll be some Injun," scowled Inky Braxton.

"Bonner Hudson'll be pleased to hear that."

A mulatto, Braxton was big all over, and not all that handy with a gun, but could stay on a green broke hoss where others got bucked off. Up until recently he'd been a lonely drifter, and he'd found that over in Utah those Mormons made short work of men of color who they considered undesirables. In Braxton's case, it was riding off with one of the five wives married to a Mormon settler. There is no greater fury, as he found out, than a pack of vengeance-minded sons of Brigham Young. The chase had been long and hard, and there he'd been beating a track up the barren Tule Valley with nothing ahead but a gap through the bristling hills and beyond that the Great Salt Lake Desert. Then salvation came in the unexpected appearance of the Kid and his gang, who'd helped to send a few Mormons to their Promised Land. He didn't know at the time that a posse was hot after Kid LaDuke.

LaDuke had a way of clicking his teeth together and chuckling, and he had the quick, sure movements of youth. That he was wanted for murder, of the gunsmith's daughters and two more since then, were just unfortunate happenings. Back at Lone Tree, evidence had been found tying in the Kid and his chums to those killings. Then later on it had been Orville Newton claiming the only one he'd killed was gunsmith Clive Brewster. Now Ol' Orville and all of his old chums were dead, but still back in the Flathead Valley was longtime lawman Harvey Black, one reason the Kid hadn't ventured back there, but not the only one. For if he did return,

13

there would also be Bonner Hudson hooking up to track him down.

The Kid dropped his eyes to the newspaper spread out before him on the table, and into them came a challenging glimmer. Along with the race-horse, Dancy Stuart had a lot of purebred stock. Some years ago a trio of Stuart's hands had come upon him where the eastern fringes of Stuart's Double S ranch swept up into the Missions. It had been the Kid and Bonner Hudson's son out doing some tracking, a pair of twelve-year-olds, a dog, and a single-action rifle. Stuart's men used the rifle to beat the dog to death and then smashed it over rocks before cuffing both him and the Hudson kid around. The final indignity had been those waddies ordering both of the boys to peel off their shoes and clothes. It was still a vivid memory, making it down off the Missions about half frozen and na-ked, feet cut and bleeding, but swearing revenge someday—

"This other part interests me," murmured the Kid. "About that challenge race to be held over at Butte. If Dancy Stuart paid all that much for that hoss, Daredevil, I'll bet he'll wager a helluva lot more that his hoss wins."

"Watta you driving at?"

"I'm homesick is what I'm drivin' at. Here"—impulsively Kid LaDuke picked some folding money and threw it so that it fluttered onto the floor—"a coupla more hundred to keep these drinks coming." He jabbed a pleased finger at the newspaper.

14

"Stealin' this Daredevil is gonna be a lot more profitable than bustin' our asses robbin' Mormon banks."

"Then what, sell that racehoss?"

"Hell no, Wiley. I figure Dancy Stuart will pay, say forty grand, to get his hoss back."

"What if he don't pay?"

"Then we'll tell the sonofabitch where he can find a dead racehoss."

Kid LaDuke had never been partial to wide open places like the Snake River Plains. As he crossed them, he'd been wary of running into more sons of Brigham Young, and not only Mormons, but the lawmen who had a habit of coming through in search of outlaws. So it was with a sense of relief that he forded the Big Lost River on the first leg of his homeward journey.

North of here it would be nothing but one mountain range after another, with high valleys and rivers in between. With the Kid were the mulatto and Wiley Sheldon. What he'd done had been to split up his gang, these three going a day ahead, and the other four remaining a day after the Kid had pulled out of Owyhee. They'd rendezvous up in Idaho at North Fork, a mountain town where the Salmon River started to make that southern loop.

Hedging around the three riders were lower peaks cutting some of the wind away, and the narrowing river delta filled with waters rippling in their back-

15

trail. The Kid knew that a few miles ahead they'd reach Mackay, a riverbank town whose bank they knew intimately, situated below higher Leatherman Peak. He mentioned this to the others as he took in Wiley Sheldon sucking on a bottle of whiskey.

"You weren't with us then, Inky."

"Maybe you two should ride in there ahead of me," said Braxton.

"I told Cunny and the others to bypass the town."

"Cunny hates to take orders," Wiley threw in.

"Especially from a wet-nosed kid such as me, I reckon," LaDuke muttered. "But he don't mind usin' his shootin' iron, so what the hell." He took off his Stetson and beat the dust from a shirtsleeve. "Awful damned dusty back there. An' it's still a far piece to where we're going. We could wash off down by the river, make camp there too. But you know, there's this boardinghouse the outskirts of town . . . well . . ."

Braxton took in the reckless glint in the Kid's eyes, and he shook his head and replied, "You sure the hell ain't bashful, Kid. I ain't never seen so many Wanteds out on one man, clear down in Texas . . . and that town ahead, I expect they'll even have some on church bulletin boards, the town library. What other attractions does this boardinghouse have other than a hot bath."

"Carrie."

It proved out, in the Kid's words, that Carrie Rindahl still had the hots for him. It wouldn't do but the Kid had to share her bedroom. A widow woman in her early thirties, she'd found out only a week ago from a fortune-teller that she was about to come into a considerable amount of money. One look at Kid LaDuke and from her kitchen window she'd let out a shriek of joy, as all Carrie Rindahl could set her mind on was the reward money out on the Kid and his accomplices. But it wasn't until sometime before sunup that she figured it safe enough to sneak out of her bedroom clothed only in her robe and her intentions of rousing the town marshal.

"Going someplace?"

"Damn you, nigger!"

Braxton's thrown fist catapulted her through the back screen door and into her kitchen. Following her in, he allowed a wide grin to lighten up his face as just for good measure he brought his boot heel down hard on her outflung hand in passing. The only thing that moved were the creaking floorboards as Braxton went up to roust the Kid and Wiley Sheldon. "Just proves you're famous, Kid," was the only comment Inky Braxton made during their passage upriver.

The one precaution they'd taken was to cut the telegraph line just south of Mackay and again a short distance to the north. From here on the road was more of a track, as in this narrow valley there were only a couple of settlements. There were three other valley passages fingering up to North Fork backgrounded by the Salmon River range.

17

The closer they got to North Fork in the waning hours of the afternoon, the more Kid LaDuke began to get the chippy glint in his eyes, and he knocked off the small talk. When they were riding in close to the river and on a stretch of washed-out road, big black flies swarmed around to nip at them. The horses wanted to run, but the last thing any of them wanted was to run into some lawmen while they sat tired horses. Further ahead the Kid could see where part of the valley they were in sideswiped northeasterly to the high rocks beyond, which would be Lost Trail Pass. Beyond that lay Montana and a lot of bad memories.

"Can't turn back now," came his determined refrain. "Bonner or Sheriff Black or whatever." Wiley and the mulatto, he mused, they don't know how damned good Bonner Hudson is. Back some, a year, maybe, it had come down to him in Nevada about the sheriff boasting that if the Kid ever came back there'd be a public hanging and another unmarked grave in the Pablo cemetery. This had been eating at LaDuke, and maybe he was only using this ploy to steal that racehorse just to return to the Flathead Valley. "Come back just to make that damned sheriff eat crow."

"Pretty soon, Kid, you're gonna start answerin' yourself."

He jerked his head to shake a few flies away from around his face and eyed Inky Braxton. The Kid grinned. "I guess she didn't have the hots for me after all."

18

"To her you were money on the hoof." A while later he added, "North Fork don't look all that big."

"Just another watering hole where if you mind your manners, the town marshal'll turn a blind eye. Just to make sure, I grease his palm."

"Kid, have you thought about how we're going to pull this off?"

"Ever since I seen that newspaper article. It isn't rustling that hoss of Dancy Stuart's so much. It's getting away afterwards, as I know Dancy will be pissed something fierce when he finds it's me stealing his racehoss. Figger he'll hire Bonner Hudson to help track us down. But, I've got this idea about that."

Chapter Two

Longtime Double S foreman Toby Earle had always been firm in his opinion that any good cutting horse could beat one of those eastern thoroughbreds. That is, until the racehorse Dancy Stuart had brought back from Kentucky simply ran away from some damned good Double S broncs. The track was a half-mile oval hedging around the home buildings, used up until now to get that Kentucky horse Daredevil accustomed to the thinner air of this mountain valley.

He'd been informed of Dancy's intentions to race Daredevil over at Butte's Columbia Gardens racetrack, which had suited Earle, as that Butte town was some wild place. As a tune-up to this, Dancy Stuart had accepted a challenge from Bisby Turner up at Eureka, Turner's Canadian horse taking on Daredevil here at the ranch. This hadn't set well with Toby Earle. Since Monday, people had been coming out, to bunk down at the main house or in the bunkhouse, and they had to be fed too, the reason one of the chuck wagons was being used. This rankled the foreman of the Double S as a lot of regular chores would have to be let go.

In what daylight there was left he could make out a buggy coming in on the main road to Big Rock, and some distance behind the buggy were three horsemen. "They'd best have bedrolls as we're full up," Toby Earle snapped cantankerously, as he kept to the shadows of an oak tree in passing a corral. Earle was rawboned and gaunt of face. He had his old worn Stetson wedged low to push out his ears some, one cheek bulged out with chewing tobacco, his attention drawn now to flames coming from a pit behind one of the hip-roofed barns. To his right and out in the yard buggies were lined up. A few men stood by them passing around bottles. Then he saw the black man off by his lonesome.

Mingled in with valley folks were the usual assortment of strangers, but he wasn't partial to blacks, and neither was Dancy Stuart. Earle began working the chaw around in his mouth, not wanting to make a row, but his resentment building. There came an unexpected smile from Inky Braxton and a friendly, "Evening, suh."

Caught by surprise, Toby Earle responded with a scowl that carried him around a shed wall.

"A tough old bird," muttered Braxton. "Brought up to hate, but never bothered to ask why." He stood there in the deeper shadow cast by a barn wall, with one boot propped up on the seat of a hand grinder. Being something of a wanderer, he could appreciate a place like this located out here on the valley floor. Southerly lay Flathead Lake, and there were plenty of streams and thick grass and timbered passages where livestock could graze, with more lakes up in the encircling peaks.

He smiled now at the Kid's precaution of bypassing Missoula, where they headed east to Clearwater and worked their way up the Swan River valley to come out south of Big Rock around midafternoon. They'd holed up in a mountain canyon from whose elevations the Flathead Lake and the northern reaches of the valley opened up to them. When the two men the Kid had sent into Big Rock returned, they learned all about that high stakes horserace.

Ike Braxton had been just another stranger coming out to Dancy Stuart's ranch. The rest of the gang trailed out in scattered bunches. And as darkness settled in, Braxton figured Kid LaDuke should be arriving soon. Smoke drifting by from the pit behind the barn brought the aroma of beef. He became aware of a shadow drifting his way.

In that curiously high-pitched voice of his, Wiley Sheldon said, "If I was a pickpocket I'd work this crowd. Must be three, four hundred out here. That hoss . . . that Daredevil, more than I expected."

"Big and black and kind of high-strung. Could be me, if I was a horse. Seen the Kid?"

"Oh, he'll be along. There's gonna be a dance in that other barn."

"For you white folks," chortled Braxton, with just a trace of bitterness in his voice. "A lot of money's being wagered. Too bad there ain't gonna be no race."

Across the wide expanse of ranch yard the owner of the Double S was holding court at a poker table. There was an ample supply of liquor and food on side tables, and some windows had been opened to let out cigar smoke. Nobody crowded around the table, as only those in the game were allowed in here. Except for Sheriff Harvey Black, the others were ranchers, and also in the game was Bisby Turner.

"I have to agree with you, Bisby, your hoss comes from good stock."

"Gallant Star, as you know, boys, has set a lot of Canadian records. So I just couldn't pass up Dancy's invite."

"Seems to me," Dancy Stuart said chidingly, "you threw down the gauntlet." Dancy was a rip-cord lean man in his late thirties. The amused grin held to his angular face, as this repartee was a part of horse racing he'd come to enjoy. He was by reputation a hard taskmaster, and it was a common sight to see a cowhand drawing his pay and taking that long road to Big Rock to look for other work. He was a grudging loser when it came to cards, was always looking to get even when that happened. Though Dancy Stuart was a familiar figure at Montana racetracks, he'd never owned a racehorse before. But when he did decide to buy one, he took the train down into Kentucky.

He knew the times turned in by Bisby Turner's Canadian horse, and it was only right that Turner be shown track records and newspaper clippings citing just what Daredevil could do. But it hadn't cost Dancy Stuart all that much to have some bogus newspaper articles made up which shaved a few seconds off Daredevil's best times, the same for records kept by the previous owner. His instructions for tomorrow's race were for the man astride Daredevil to barely edge out Turner's horse, as he knew the results of the race would be carried over to Butte. It wasn't cheating, in Dancy's opinion, but just the way business was carried out.

"Fifty?" One of the ranchers took a keen look at Bisby Turner. "Bisby, are you bluffing again?"

"Ed, if I were you'd be the first man I'd tell."

"Bonner's due back most any day."

Dancy Stuart threw a distracted glance at the sheriff. "Bonner Hudson?"

Sheriff Harvey Black folded his cards and replied, "Boys over in Idaho needed help in tracking down some rustlers."

This got Dancy Stuart to remembering that his oldest son was going to marry Bonner's daughter. The thought irritated him, as he didn't entirely approve of this marriage. But it was like Harvey

24

Black to throw in an aside like this and get a man off his feed. As for Lillian Hudson, Stuart supposed she was pretty enough, but there was Bonner, the last of a dying breed called tracker. Some called him other things: bounty hunter, mountain man, even renegade. But this was 1879, a time when a man staked his claim to land. No question about it, mused Stuart, Bonner Hudson would be an eyesore as a father-in-law to his son, Kelsay. Damn, Kimball here has a couple of eligible daughters.

"Dancy, you in?"

"Yeah, yeah, sure."

Kid LaDuke loped his horse around some grazing cattle, and there was some hesitation when he came over a rise and took in the home buildings of the Double S. It was as he remembered, the two big barns and Dancy Stuart's rambling ranch house hewed out of Engelmann spruce logs. There was a flurry of sparks from a big fire out behind one of the barns, and in the glare of it he could make out people lined up by two tables placed end to end. Sprinkled around the yard were a lot of lanterns, and a quick tally told the Kid at least a couple of hundred had come in for tomorrow's race.

"Only there ain't gonna be any race," said Kid LaDuke with a grin. It was a bold move, him coming out here, as a lot out here would probably know him, even though he'd beefed up a little and had started to grow chin whiskers.

There was a high bluff this side of the buildings where in the deeper darkness below a creek wandered southward toward Flathead Lake, and the Kid skirted away from the buildings. A cut in the bluff, worn by livestock, took the Kid down onto a ribbon of loamy bank hardened from lack of rain. Further up the creek, backlighted by the nearby lights in the ranch yard, some men rose from where they'd been taking their ease on a fallen cottonwood, while the Kid dismounted to walk his horse over there.

"About time," muttered Cunny.

"Only around eleven or so," said the Kid. "How does it look?"

"They've got that racehoss in the other barn. Early yet, so I don't know what the setup'll be. But a couple of waddies are in there now."

"Shouldn't have any trouble. As the last person good ol' Dancy expects to attend his little shindig is me."

"One thing, Kid, earlier I saw this gent packing a badge. Big fellow, dark-haired."

"That'll be the sheriff," said the Kid as his eyes lighted up, and he laughed. "Harvey Black being out here makes it that much better." He unbuttoned a shirt pocket and pulled out a folded sheet of paper, which proved to be a Wanted poster with a picture of the Kid. He read what he'd written on the back, "Your racehoss stolen compliments of

the Kid LaDuke gang. You want Daredevil back
. . . expect to fork out forty thousand . . . or your
hoss'll suffer the consequences." Some of the
words had been misspelled, but the intent was
clear, and smiles broke out.

"You said we make our move sometime after
midnight."

"Yup, Cunny, the moon'll be down by then.
Waiting any longer will only bring mornin' that
much quicker. As by sunup I want to be up in the
Missions. Clouding up some too, which'll help.
That fiddle music?"

"Got a dance goin' on in one of the barns."

Back when he first sighted the buildings, Kid
LaDuke had also noticed some campfires scattered
about, the men by them spreading out bedrolls,
and there were a few out exercising their horses on
the oval track. Now he issued orders for his hardcases to go in singly or paired up, and to circle
around so's to come in where there was this grove
of trees behind the south barn. "Tie up your
hosses there. 'Cause that's where I told Braxton
and Wiley to leave their mounts. So, that leaves us
about an hour to partake of Dancy's hospitality."

The last to leave the haven of the creek was Kid
LaDuke, on foot, walking his horse, which was
patched with white-and-black coloring and didn't
tire easily. Closing in to where light was driving
back the night, the Kid tugged his hat lower, along
with pulling up the collar of his leather coat. He
avoided gazing directly at campfires and skirted

27

lanterns pegged on poles, but he couldn't help noticing, to his immense pleasure, that he recognized a lot of people. As he passed an open-sided smitty's shop, a voice came from behind, "Watch your backside, Kid."

Just for a moment he froze, but got his grin working again as he said, "Where's Braxton?"

Wiley Sheldon fell into step. "Making a hog of hisself over at that barbecue pit. Looks good; just two watching that racehoss . . . and about everybody else gettin' boozed to the gills."

"Seen Mr. Dancy Stuart?"

"From what I hear he's camped out in the main house."

"Got a game going. Which is where Black'll be too."

"I've been thinking, Kid." He took a wary backward glance as they cleared the last barn to find a side wall. "That other hoss could turn us a profit too."

"Nope, Wiley, put that notion to bed. Just Dancy's hoss is all we want. We get greedy and . . ."

The Kid had made it clear that if any of his men weren't out by the horses at midnight they'd be left behind. And by midnight the party hadn't lost stride, which suited the Kid's purpose. From the haven of the grove of trees the outlaws checked their saddle rigging, and a short distance away a woman and a cowhand appeared briefly as they scurried toward some bushes. Then the Kid's voice brought their eyes to him.

"Me and Cunny and Braxton are going in." The Kid threw his reins to Wiley Sheldon.

"Here comes someone else."

The Kid took in a man moving up to the back double doors of the barn, and he said, "That's Toby Earle, foreman out here. He's goin' in, probably to check on things. Won't change our plans any. Come on."

In a whispery voice Inky Braxton said, "Leave this Toby Earle to me."

By the high back wall of the barn, Kid LaDuke lifted the door latch and was the first to enter the barn. There was the middle runway and the stalls lining it, and further along lantern light coming out of one stall and a raspy voice he knew as Toby Earle's. He motioned for Cunny to ease over. Trailed by Braxton, the Kid unleathered a six-gun, as all of them slinked along quiet as they could. If there was trouble, it would come from Toby Earle.

The horses in the stalls they passed stirred but otherwise kept munching at hay thrown down from the loft. It was Toby Earle chawing away at those with him that the Kid honed in on. "Don't give him any more grain now," Earle went on. "Anybody comes in, send them packin', Murdock, or you'll be lookin' for a place to work."

"What the hell, Toby, you don't have ta be so testy."

"Just do it," the foreman shot back, and he came out of the stall, leaving Murdock and another hand behind. Then Toby Earle felt night air stabbing into the barn, and he took in the open back door and the vague outline of the hardcase Cunny. It didn't make sense at first, Cunny standing back there, but now the foreman of the Double S saw the gun the intruder held, and just like that Earle broke toward the front doors, as he and the waddies watching Daredevil weren't packing iron.

Before the Kid could think to use his gun, there came a whirring sound past his head. The knife thrown by Inky Braxton plunged in between the foreman's shoulder blades, and as Earle tumbled into the gutter between the runway and the back of a stall, Kid LaDuke made his presence known to the other Double S hands.

"Don't even think of using that pitchfork! You didn't like that sonofabitchin' Toby Earle anyway. Untie that halter rope."

"You . . . you're LaDuke?"

"None other. Cunny, latch on to that halter rope. Awright, boys, squat down."

"Please, don't kill us, Kid . . . take . . . take the hoss. . . ."

"Here." The Kid let the Reward poster flutter down in front of the kneeling men, their backs to him and an eager grin washing across the Kid's face. He eased to one side as Inky Braxton came into the stall reversing the grip on his six-gun. "Just be sure and give that paper to Dancy." At his nod, their weapons slashed out and struck skull bone.

30

Quickly Braxton went to retrieve his knife as the racehorse caught the scent of blood and reared up, but the Kid was there to tie another rope onto the halter. Once it was outside, the horse quieted down, with the other hardcases saddledbound and coming in. Vaulting into the saddle, Kid LaDuke let one of the other hardcases take charge of the halter rope. He brought them, as they'd planned, westerly where there were more trees, the ground dipping away and shielding them from the buildings. From here they'd head north to an encirclement route the Kid knew would carry them into the mountains.

"Went damned slick, Kid."

"I almost regret havin' to take out Toby Earle."

"I don't," the mulatto muttered.

"You said there was somethin' else we had to do?"

"Yeah, Wiley, there is. But that ain't gonna happen until early tomorrow. Awright, let's stretch out our hosses some."

Chapter Three

"It was your brag, Sheriff, that you'd hang La-Duke if he came back." There was a controlled fury in Dancy Stuart's voice. He'd been shown the Reward poster left by Kid LaDuke. But to Dancy it was more than his foreman getting killed, it was the humiliation of having someone walk right in here and steal Daredevil.

"Be hard picking up their trail tonight."

"The hell it will," Stuart flung back at Sheriff Harvey Black. "Roust the hands, Murdock."

Sheriff Black had learned long ago one didn't argue common sense with rancher Dancy Stuart. Back a spell Dancy had been struggling to hang on like everyone else out here in the Flathead Valley. Then came a large inheritance from an eastern relative, which brought Dancy's elevation from a hardscrabble rancher to the largest landowner out here. One thing Dancy couldn't buy was friends, and he didn't have all that many to start with, but maybe it didn't matter as Dancy seemed to thrive on the hatred of his many enemies. There were quite a few come out just to see Dancy's horse get beat tomorrow. Could be, mused Harvey Black, they'd derive some satisfaction out of LaDuke stealing that racehorse.

The tracks left by the outlaws heading out from behind the barn were picked up right away, and now Stuart and his waddies and Sheriff Black followed the tracks out northerly beyond the buildings. It was sometime after three o'clock, the night still holding sway. With just starlight to help them pick out random hoof markings, they had to hold at a lope.

Harvey Black could have ridden up amongst the pack of riders, but he held near the back, because it would do no good at this point to tell Dancy Stuart those outlaws would break toward the Missions. A lead rider felt his horse slipping out from under him, but he managed to rein it in, as he shouted back, "Damn near rode into a bog; must be near Caribou creek."

Now the riders began milling around. They looked to Dancy Stuart for leadership, and Dancy yelled, "Those bastards must have doubled back. Bet they're heading for the Missions." He brought his horse back and fell in alongside the sheriff. Dancy's accusing words drove a wedge between them: "You had this figured out."

"That the Kid would head up into the mountains. There's peaks to either side, Mr. Stuart. And La-Duke knows every damned washout and cave and canyon in them way back into Idaho. But you forgot something . . ."

"What now?"

"That you won't fork over a dime for a dead racehoss."

The sheriff and the others were forking tired horses when on a lifting foothill they surveyed a canyon running deep into the Missions. By chance some two hours back they picked up the tracks left by the Kid and his bunch, and Dancy Stuart pulled back sharply on his reins. The curses of the rancher echoed up into the canyon as Stuart vented his anger and frustration.

At least, came Sheriff Black's sobering thought, Stuart knows enough not to keep after the Kid. In the first place, none of them were trackers of the Kid's caliber, and right about now LaDuke and his gang were probably up there having a laugh over this. Stealing a horse was one thing, but to kill Toby Earle. Why hadn't the Kid killed the others who were there? As had been the case back at Lone Tree, that gunsmith and his daughters. That the Kid was still riding the outlaw trail meant to Harvey Black he had failed as a lawman. Every time he came across a Wanted on the Kid it was a bitter reminder of this.

Around them was a lifting grayness and it was dead still, that hushed time before day broke across the valley. Everyone knew they had to turn back, since any venturing into the Missions for any length of time required they get bedrolls and supplies. They were, by Black's estimation, about twenty-five miles east of the Double S home buildings, but he wouldn't be going there; he'd be going back to Big Rock, and he voiced this to Dancy Stuart.

"I'll try to get up a posse."

"Try isn't good enough, Harv. I not only want my horse back, I want the Kid dead."

"Not as much as I do," said the sheriff. "All of the Kid's old chums are dead. Only reason he's alive is 'cause LaDuke knows these mountains."

"Not as good as Bonner Hudson," said Stuart. "You tell Bonner I want to hire him on to track down LaDuke. Tell him I don't give a damn how much it costs. You tell Bonner that."

"You fixin' to come along?"

Dancy Stuart sent cold eyes sweeping up the canyon to sunlight beginning to touch on the higher reaches of the Missions. You could tell he was a proud man the way he sat in the saddle; there was an aloofness about him that kept a lot at bay. "You ought to know by now"—Dancy's words cut viciously at everyone there—"nobody steals from me. You tell Bonner to wait at Big Rock for me."

Just riding away from Dancy Stuart and his Double S hands made Sheriff Harvey Black feel a lot easier. As he rode, he discarded any notions that once they struck out after Kid LaDuke the letter of the law would be observed. Dancy Stuart, he wanted the Kid dead, not so much to avenge his foreman getting killed, but out of sheer arrogance, because just maybe Dancy considered himself above the law.

What about Sheriff Black? Did capturing the Kid alive fit into his plans? There would be some vindication in a public hanging, the Kid and the rest of those hardcases. To just hang on as sheriff simply

35

wasn't enough, not when the Kid came back to throw the past into his face. He was getting on, into his late forties. It would be good to hang up his badge knowing it had been Harvey Black bringing in Kid LaDuke. *At least,* he thought, *my pride'll be restored.*

The key to this, he felt, was Bonner Hudson. For Bonner it was a case of betrayed trust. He'd shown the Kid the mysteries of tracking, and of staying alive in this high country where a lot of folks perished. Bonner never killed when he didn't have to, nor was he someone you pushed around. Now the sheriff's worry was that Bonner Hudson could decide to stay out of this. That would leave him nursing what posse he could throw together and Dancy Stuart in high places where Kid LaDuke would have the decided edge.

If Dancy was smart he'd pack along the ransom money the Kid wants for that racehorse, the sheriff thought. He just hoped Bonner Hudson got back in the next day or two. Otherwise they'd be following a lot of false trails up there.

Further south and on the lower reaches of the Mission range flanking Flathead Valley, there was a boisterous optimism amongst the outlaws. Boldly they had a large campfire going, the smoke from it drifting through a copse of shivering aspens. The Kid had held back from reaming out Braxton for using his knife. Killing Dancy Stuart's segundo had added insult to injury, and it let the rancher know the same thing could happen to his thoroughbred,

Daredevil, which was tethered downwind with the other horses.

It was warm enough now to shuck their outergarments. Kid LaDuke took off his leather coat and folded it to place in his bedroll, which he rolled up and tossed by his saddle. Gaining possession of the racehorse and getting away with it clean, had added to the Kid's stature. Now he would have to explain that the hard part was coming up.

"Listen up," he said loudly as he held out his tin cup to Wiley Sheldon, who was pouring coffee out of a blackened pot.

"Hey, Wiley, don't give all of it away."

"What's up, Kid?"

"Trouble for us if we don't handle this right. We've more or less kidnapped that rancher's hoss. But it ain't Dancy Stuart worries me as much as another gent living hereabouts."

"I reckon you told us about this Bonner Hudson."

"That's who I'm talking about, Cunny. I want Bonner to come after us. I figure Dancy Stuart'll try to hire Bonner to track us down. The sheriff figures in this too. Which means there'll be more of them than us."

"Why don't we just take that hoss east, to Butte maybe, and sell the damned thing. Should get considerable for it."

"Nobody with half a brain will shell out a dime for that hoss, even if we was to present a bill of sale. Nope, I want Dancy's money. Which is why we're gonna kidnap Bonner's daughter."

"Be saddled with some snot-nosed girl? Don't make sense, Kid?"

"His girl Lillian is gonna be our insurance policy. I want them to catch up to us, but we'll give them a helluva run before that happens. The deal is Dancy gives us the forty thousand, he gets his hoss back. But we keep the girl . . ."

"Yeah, they either let us get away or she dies."

"Well, Cunny?"

The outlaw Cunny took up the challenge he saw in Kid LaDuke's eyes. He was at least fifteen years older, had let this resentment build over having to take orders from a fuzzy-cheeked yonker. The Kid had been on a roll down in Utah and Nevada, but this was a heap different from robbing banks. At the moment he was clever enough not to buck the Kid, and he let the moment pass. Down the trail someone as young as this was bound to make a mistake. Then he'd be there to take over, and if the Kid was stupid enough to try and match his draw, that suited Cunny all the more.

"Kid," he said amiably, "when someone's playing a hot hand you leave pretty much alone. I like the idea of some added insurance. Just where does this Bonner live?"

"Couple of miles further south and down in the foothills. It won't be that easy getting in there, so we'll play it this way."

Chapter Four

Over the years Angelica Hudson had come to accept the long absences of her husband. When they were first married there were times she considered leaving Bonner, even though they had the one child. She'd felt this mountain cabin was no place to raise Lillian, where it would often be weeks before someone passed by. Later on a son was born, and by then Angelica Hudson knew this place of splendid isolation was home.

Home was just inside the mouth of a canyon near the northern reaches of the Missions. The cabin contained four rooms and a covered front porch, with stone steps plunging down from it to a wide pond hemmed in by reeds. The pond was joined to a mountain stream surging over huge rocks. The one trail in was from the east and under huge pines, and Angelica Hudson looked toward it now, scanning the open reaches beyond the mouth of the canyon. Her eyes were filled with the expected arrival of her husband.

Still willowy at thirty-five, she wore one of Bon-

ner's old shirts, the sleeves rolled up past her el-
bows, and form-fitting Levi's and moccasins. Sunlight struck down through sheltering pines to touch
the burnished head of chestnut hair and to high-
light the tanned face bare of makeup. She wore
her hair in braids tied with red ribbons; her left
hand was curled around the lower handle of an
ax. Taking their ease in shadows by the woodpile
were two dogs, a collie and a golden retriever that
Bonner had given to Lillian when it was a puppy.
But Lillian had, for the last three years, been away
at school during the winters, and now the retriever,
Missy, had distanced itself.

Lillian was engaged to Kelsay Stuart, and it had
changed her. As she leaned to position a hunk of
wood on a cutting block, Angelica Hudson realized that her daughter had lost her love for this
place. Going to school in a valley town would do
that, she knew. And when she did send her daughter out to gain an education, Angelica knew part
of it would be Lillian's meeting a lot of young
men. She's far too pretty for her own good, came
another wistful thought. Then Angelica brought
the ax down to cleave the hunk of wood in half as
her daughter called out.

"Mother!"

She turned to look at Lillian, who held a blouse
out an open window. "Yes, I'll sew a button on it,
but we do need firewood." Another point of worry
to Angelica was of her daughter getting a summer
job over at Big Rock. This was a ploy so Lillian
could be closer to Kelsay Stuart and her school

friends. That Bonner had agreed to let their daughter take the job had come as a surprise.

The collie barking and springing up brought Angelica's eyes to the downsloping trail. Sometimes Bonner Hudson liked to ease in without being seen, and an expectant smile graced her full lips. Only when the retriever started growling did it occur to her that it could be someone other than her husband. Or, as it sometimes happened out here, a grizzly passing through.

"Hush," she called to the dogs, as within Angelica Hudson rose this wary feeling. In the shed just west of the house there was a rifle, but the house was closer and another rifle leaned by the open front door. She held by the woodpile, doing as Bonner had showed her, just holding quietly to one spot to let the canyon speak, the throaty murmuring of the creek, the wind a distant wail above the canyon walls. Then some birds suddenly rose up lower in the canyon, and she knew there was an alien intrusion. Calmly, she sank the ax blade into the chopping block and started upslope toward the front porch.

"Hello the house!"

Turning slightly as she walked, Angelica Hudson searched along the downsloping trail until she could make out the shadowy outline of a horseman. "I know that voice," she murmured, and added in a louder tone to her daughter, "Seems we've got company." She stepped onto the porch, would have held there had not the dogs wheeled to break toward the creek and away from the incoming horseman. While the collie held to the near bank, the retriever splashed across the creek and began yowling. Leaning in the door, Angelica picked up the rifle as the rider called out again,

"Mrs. Hudson . . . it's me . . . Teddy La-Duke . . ."

"I'll be damned . . ." Questions dancing in her eyes, she levered the Winchester while moving out toward the porch steps.

"Teddy LaDuke is here?"

"Stay in the house, honey."

Still a considerable distance out, the Kid drew rein as with the other hand he waved at Angelica Hudson. "I decided to come back, Mrs. Hudson . . . to give myself up. Just gettin' tired of running. Just wanted to talk to Bonner first . . ." He removed his hat, to show his face better and to wipe the sweat from his forehead.

"Are you alone?"

"Been alone a long time. Hot out here in the sun."

"I expect Bonner to ride in most anytime, Teddy."

"I know what they say about me . . . that I killed those girls over to Lone Tree. But I swear on my mother's grave, Mrs. Hudson, it weren't me but Orville done the killing. You say Bonner's due most any time? Just to ease your mind . . . I reckon I can wait out here . . . over there by the creek as my hoss needs watering . . ."

"That was awful rude of you, Mom, not inviting Teddy up to the house."

She turned to gaze upon her daughter framed in the doorway, at the long strands of light brown hair and realized it wasn't just her daughter anymore but a young and desirable woman of eighteen. And about now all Angelica Hudson could set her mind on was what had happened to those two girls over at Lone Tree. It was the dogs still yammering away at something beyond the creek that told her Teddy LaDuke wasn't alone, that steeled her impulse to get the other rifle out of the shed. She crossed to the door.

Coldly, firmly she said to Lillian, "Listen to me. He isn't alone. Take the rifle. You cover me when I go to the shed to get the other rifle. Whatever happens, don't leave the house."

"Mom, Teddy won't dare harm us."

"No more than he wouldn't hurt those other girls. Cover me." Angelica Hudson padded around and came off the porch, glancing at Kid LaDuke down by the creek with his back to her as he stood by his horse, which was lapping up water. The collie turned and started toward her, but spun back toward the creek, a deep snarl of warning in its throat. Somehow she got the shed door open, and with a sign of relief she reached in to pick up the rifle. In turning back her pace quickened. Then the rifle seemed to spin out of her hands. A stinging pain went up her arm, and the sound of the bullet scared up a lot of birds. She broke running for the house, only to be confronted by two men swinging around a shed wall, and she screamed, "Lillian, barricade the door!"

In the house, a confused Lillian Hudson saw three men materialize from brush beyond the creek. They killed the retriever first, then began peppering shots at the collie. The next thing that came into Lillian's limited range of vision where she stood just inside the door was Inky Braxton, and she cried out, "Stop, stop . . . or I'll shoot . . ."

"You do an' we kill your ma. Throw out that rifle."

"No!" screamed Angelica, "Keep the rifle!"

One of the hardcases lashed out with the barrel of his handgun. The force of the blow tumbled Angelica Hudson against the shed wall, where she crumpled down, and the mulatto stepped boldly onto the porch. He smiled at the young woman inside; she lowered the rifle barrel, then his arm lashed out and grabbed it. He brushed by Lillian to check about for more weapons.

Riding up now was Kid LaDuke, as the rest of the hardcases came into view. The smile showed that the Kid felt good about how things had gone. He got down to groundhitch his reins, and then, still smiling, he held out his arms and said, "Well, Lily, ain't you gonna give me a welcome home hug . . ."

Wiley Sheldon grinned. "Reckon she ain't, Kid. But she's prettier than you made her out to be . . . damned pretty."

"Why are you doing this?" Lillian asked through her tears as she came off the porch, and then she hurried toward her mother lying by the shed.

"Women," the Kid blurted out, "they always got to have answers to everything. She'll find out soon enough." There was another shed, and a smoke-house, and deeper against the canyon wall a corral occupied by three horses. The Kid's plans were to overnight here. But when they pulled out, those horses of Bonner Hudson's would be coming along packing supplies and his daughter aboard one of them.

It had been a few years, but as Kid LaDuke's glance took in the upper reaches of the canyon, he recalled the many times he'd been up there, and pretty much throughout the Missions. He'd become Bonner Hudson's second son, but, he mused as a smile flickered, Bonner'd be calling him a sonofabitch once he found out about this.

"Hey, Lily, you've got a hungry bunch of men on your hands. So head in there and rustle up some grub." He ambled over to the shed and added, "I'll tend to your ma."

"Damn you, Teddy," Lillian Hudson said angrily. "Why can't you leave us alone."

He pulled her to her feet, gave her a shove that sent Lillian reeling toward the house as he said, "Don't you know, Lily honey, you're my ace in the hole. Wiley, get her out of here, then bring back some water."

"It would be a lot simpler, Kid," said one of the hardcases, "just to wait here until Hudson pulls in an' then kill him."

"We'll do it my way," said Kid LaDuke.

"And what way is that, Teddy?"

He swiveled his head around to gaze at Angelica Hudson staring back at him around the blood trickling down her forehead and around the bridge of her nose. She had pushed to a sitting position, and then had reached to press her left arm against her side, suppressing the pain she felt, and hiding her fear from LaDuke and the others. Around a grin he shook his head as he hunkered down.

"You never did really cotton to me."

In her brutally honest way Angelica Hudson replied, "I've never liked sneak thiefs, which you were then, Teddy."

The Kid's face crimsoning, he glanced around as his mouth became an ugly line. "You always were damned blunt. I should kill you, Mrs. Hudson."

"But you won't—"

"Yeah?"

"Because, Teddy, you're scared shitless of Bonner."

The Kid came unglued in a mindless word frenzy, reaching to grab Angelica Hudson by the front of her shirt. He forced her down and dropped down to straddle her waist, the words still coming out all twisted and ugly.

"When we leave in the mornin' we're takin' your bitch of a daughter along! Do you hear me! You tell Bonner that! You damned loud-mouthed bitch." He punched her alongside the head, and she went limp. "Lock her in the shed. You, Wiley, Bonner always keeps some whiskey around; up at the house. Damned bitch anyway." Rising, he sucked angry air into his lungs.

* * *

Sometime before dawn Angelica Hudson awoke to find that the outlaws were gone. Providently they had unlocked the shed door, and she came staggering out to stare up at the house just beginning to be besieged with flames. "Oh . . . no? Why . . . LaDuke, you inhuman bastard . . ." Hatred, along with the fear too that her daughter was with them, welled up to choke the rest of her words away.

The heat from the flames beat her downslope, and by the pond she simply dropped down. She laved icy cold water over her face, her tears mingling with the water, the sight of the dead collie beyond the pool making her forget her own pain. Slaking her thirst helped to bring back her usual calm way of thinking. With this came the realization it was cold, possibly in the low thirties, and that in the shed she'd find clothing stored away for the summer.

"Can't stay and wait for Bonner. Have to walk out." That it was over thirty miles to Big Rock meant little to Angelica Hudson. The way those scum had treated her was a signal that Lillian would be accorded the same treatment, and worse. The thought of what had happened to the gunsmith's daughters brought Angelica somewhat painfully to her feet.

By the shed, when she reached out with her left hand to shove the door out of the way, Angelica realized her hand refused to turn properly. It came

47

to her that the bullet which had dislodged the rifle from her hand had also broken a bone. Through gritted teeth she used some material she found in the shed to bind her arm tightly to her chest. Clothed in a Sheepskin and a hat, and with one of Bonner's old hunting knives tucked in her waistband, she came out of the shed and gave a final look at the burning cabin as she found the outgoing trail.

"Teddy LaDuke, your big mistake was being born. For if Bonner doesn't kill you . . . I damn sure will."

Chapter Five

Since it was Kid LaDuke that had done the killing, Sheriff Harvey Black didn't have any trouble getting a posse together. But he held in Big Rock until the afternoon stage pulled in. To his disappointment Bonner Hudson wasn't on the stage, though some of those he'd sworn in wanted to take out after those outlaws.

"By now, Sheriff, LaDuke could be out of the Missions."

"Yup, Sheriff, my bones tell me rainy weather's moving in. Once that happens we'll play hell picking up the Kid's trail"

Sheriff Black looked out at them standing by their horses, which were tied in front of the jail, and across the street by Hardy's Mercantile Store. He'd told them before they'd probably have to wait for Dancy Stuart to come in, and of Dancy's intentions to hire Bonner Hudson to do the tracking. Of the fifteen men volunteering to go along, only a handful were good riders and two of them above average with a gun. The morning of the second day out would see most of them dropping out to return to Big Rock. What bothered him more than this was Dancy Stuart going along. Not that an extra gun wouldn't be needed out there, but Stuart would want to take charge.

As for Jake Fridley's bones telling him a rainstorm was moving in, there was no sky change to speak of, just a few clouds over Squaw Peak, and the usual haze hanging over other mountain ranges encircling the valley. The air was summer tangy, about as hot as it got out here, and if it hadn't have been for the Kid showing up, Sheriff Black would be taking his afternoon coffee over at Becker's Café. He squinted downstreet at a messenger boy from the telegraph office crossing at a run.

Could be from Bonner sayin' he's been held up. With a grimace the sheriff exchanged the yellow envelope for a dime he tossed the messenger boy. "Like I said, I expect Dancy Stuart to arrive shortly. For now, get out of the sun. But don't forget I've deputized you men."

Amidst some grumbling Sheriff Black tore open the envelope. "I'll be . . . the telegram's from Kid LaDuke." And though the telegram was addressed to him, the gist of what it read was meant for Dancy Stuart. Without turning he said to one of his deputies loafing in the doorway, "The Kid expects Dancy to pay forty thousand ransom for that racehorse."

"We catch the Kid he'll damnsure hang, Harv. The nerve of that killin' . . ."

"Don't say where a swap's to be made, or where

LaDuke's heading. But the last sentence, Dancy'll like this—just keep tracking me."

"What the Kid lacks in smarts he more'n makes up in brazen nerve. We gonna hold here?"

"Got no choice, I reckon, Jim Bob. LaDuke learned a lot about tracking from Bonner; more'n we'll ever know. Damn, if Bonner don't show—"

Another man filled with the expectancy of finding that Bonner Hudson had returned from Idaho rode in around sundown. The reaction from Dancy Stuart was one of suppressed anger, not so much that Bonner Hudson hadn't returned, as by the telegram from Kid LaDuke. His hands bunched into knots, the rancher ripped the telegram into shreds that littered the floor in the sheriff's office.

"I'll send him to hell first!" exploded Dancy Stuart. "Here we're sitting up here . . . and that scummy LaDuke rides big as you please into Ronan and sends that telegram."

"At least that'll be a starting point. The Kid expects us to keep tracking after him. Any of your men got experience along this line?"

"What the hell, Harv, you're the sheriff."

"I'm good, but I expect we'll be hittin' into the mountains again. Hope that horse of yours stands up to it. What I've done, Dancy, is to send my deputies on ahead down to Ronan. They should pick up the Kid's trail. Now the question is, do you want to wait for Bonner to show?"

"When's the first stage due in from the south?"

51

"Around nine tomorrow morning. Guess if Bonner ain't on it we'll have to head out."

Nodding, the rancher said sarcastically, "I expect you got a posse together . . ."

"A few cowhands, but mostly townsfolk."

"Just hope they have the same spirit to go after those outlaws after they've got a chance to think about it tonight. Those who do go, if any can't keep up, just too damned bad. In the morning, Harv."

Sheriff Harvey Black's three deputies rode into Pablo long after sundown, and decided to stay there as Ronan was just a few miles further to the south. Stabling their horses, they took their rifles and saddlebags along to the Antler Hotel, which was settled in between a vacant lot and a side street. Jim Bob Benham often took charge on these excursions when the sheriff wasn't along. Benham wasn't bossy about it; it was just his nature. He was graying and had this somber, pockmarked face, but he did manage a smile for the woman presiding over the hotel lobby.

"I expect you're after LaDuke."

"I expect you're right, Marge." He placed his rifle on the countertop. "I expect everybody in the valley knows what happened up at Dancy's place."

"If they don't they're brain dead. Just tonight?"

"Be pullin' out long before first light."

"Howdy, Grisham, Rick."

The other deputy sheriffs responded with quiet howdies, with Rick McPherson shaping a friendly grin. He was twenty-one, a cowhand until less than a year ago. And the deputies looked like ordinary cowhands but for the round badges pinned to their shirts. To Rick McPherson's dismay the last year had seen him grow another inch to an even six feet causing him to discard some old shirts. They called him Irish handsome, though his nose had been broken in a fistfight.

On the ride down from Big Rock, mostly they had discussed whether Bonner Hudson would get back in time to help them track down Kid La-Duke. He had let Walt Grisham and Jim Bob carry the load of the conversation, since he didn't want to refresh their memories that he'd been courting Bonner's daughter. That is, he had until Lily Hudson got engaged to Kelsay Stuart. It was because of Kelsay's money more than anything. He could give Lily a better life than someone drawing deputy's pay. Others had courted Lily too, as befitting one of the prettiest girls in these parts, but it had been his misfortune, Rick McPherson felt, to fall in love with her. Or maybe it was just his pride being hurt that she'd accepted Kelsay's proposal.

"You know," said Walt Grisham, "this is the Kid's hometown."

"They've still got a picture of him over at Albert's."

Grisham said to the woman, "Yeah, that baby picture of the Kid, guess pretty is only skin deep."

As they turned to the staircase, a rap at a front window held the deputies, and then the door

53

opened and a man entered, his eyes showing his excitement, "Howdy, Jim Bob, Walt . . . an' Rick. This wire just came from Camas Prairie. In passing through, those outlaws gunned down Sid Carson. Damn, Sid was a fine lawman."

"Means they're breaking into the Bitterroots," Jim Bob said worriedly.

The town marshal of Pablo said, "Fired off a wire up to Big Rock about this. Where's the sheriff?"

"Still up there. Guess we can bypass Ronan. Yeah, you're right, Carson was a good man." Walt Grisham, a stocky man with a wide face and outthrust jaw, let his eyes register how he felt. "That damned Kid LaDuke."

The way these men felt about Kid LaDuke was being shared by Angelica Hudson, dropping down on a pebbly stretch of beach of a lake still some distance south of Big Rock. She eased at a crouch out into the dark lake waters until only her head showed above the surface. The cold water was a balm to her body, which was pushed almost beyond endurance. She ducked her head under the surface and came up gasping and brushing wet hair away from her face. Before entering the water she'd removed her coat and hat and slipped the knife into a coat pocket. Then, as it occurred to her she hadn't taken off her moccasins, she said, "Just a horribly bad day."

The last traces of the Missions lay westerly. Opposite and just as close lay the saw-toothing Swan range blotting out the night sky. Emerging from the lake, she heard a drumming of hoofbeats. The fear that it was the outlaws coming after her brought her down toward the coat and hat and the knife, which she grasped while fighting back the pain lancing at her left arm. Her right eye had closed, and that side of her face was swollen.

On the barren trail leading toward Big Rock there appeared the ghostly outlines of two riders. They would have loped into the darkness of night had she not suddenly whistled. One of the horses bucked to almost throw his rider as the other horseman quartered his horse toward the lake, and Angelica Hudson cried out in a voice full of pain, "Over here . . . please . . . over here . . ."

Lining in toward the lake shoreline were the two cowhands. It wasn't until they cleared some brush that they spotted Angelica rising unsteadily to her feet, and one exclaimed, "Why, damned if it ain't Bonner's missus!"

"Rusty Wade," she said weakly, "you're a life-saver." Then she crumbled down, still clutching the knife, and determined not to pass out.

"What happened, ma'am?"

She reached out for the cowhand leaning over her, and said, "Got a courtesy call from Kid La-Duke."

"The Kid—lucky you're still alive. Look at this, Charley, he beat the hell . . . the stuffings out of Mrs. Hudson. You know, I smelled smoke up where you live, Mrs. Hudson . . ."

"Burned our place down . . . took Lillian with them . . . please, must get to Big Rock."

"Sure you can set a saddle? Maybe we should start a fire and let you get warmed up first."

"I can get warmed up in town." She struggled to her feet and was helped into the saddle, with the cowhand climbing up behind her. The horse cantering under her, she added, "That sonofabitchin' LaDuke, if he harms my daughter, so help me, Rusty."

"Should have gelded the Kid a long time ago."

"Among other things."

Chapter Six

It had been a long haul out of Idaho for Bonner Hudson, one stagecoach having broken down just outside of Clark Fork. He'd considered walking on in and buying a horse, but ahead were a lot of mountain passes and maybe some cold weather. Back sharing a jail cell at Cocolalla were some bank robbers he'd tracked down. For his part in catching them, Bonner had collected a thousand dollars, and an off-chance he might get some of the reward money.

Bonner was a deep-chested man, long of limb, and he preferred to avoid a crowd, which was the reason he was taking his ease on the roof of the Overland stagecoach. Another was that he knew the driver, from whom Bonner had found out about Kid LaDuke's coming back to commit more crimes. The Flathead Valley had opened up to them, and the patches of prairie grass on the flats sprinkled with sunlight turned Bonner Hudson's thoughts to home.

Though Angelica endured his sometimes long absences, he was considering another line of work. There were any number of ranches he could hire on at, or he could take to trapping. Just last month the U.S. marshal stationed down at Missoula had made inquiry about Bonner's becoming a deputy marshal, but taking a job of this sort would see him leaving home again.

Shotgun Virg Modahl looked back at their passenger, and what he saw was the vague reddish tint to the shaggy hair under the rolled brim of the Stetson, just below that the eyes of Bonner Hudson seeming to be looking at the fringes of the horizon. The clothing worn by the tracker was varying shades of brown, and the boots without spurs. The face was interesting, its classical features darkened by constant exposure to the high mountain plateaus, and there was a steadfast calm about Hudson too, as if all of his senses were gripped in a waiting silence. It struck Modahl that this was the last man he'd want after him if he went outside the law.

The long look from the shotgun caused Bonner Hudson to show an easy smile. "Riding these things for any length of time could see a man's hemorrhoids acting up."

"They say you've got a sense of humor."

To which the driver added, "Not when he gets bested at stud poker."

"Abe, when was the last time you beat me at cards?"

"Been a spell, Bonner, been a spell. We're about

a half hour late. Don't hear any of the passengers bitching about it, but know I'll catch hell from Smithson—now there's a gent deserves to get the piles."

It wasn't the manager of the stage station at Big Rock, though, but rancher Dancy Stuart who'd been barely able to restrain his temper over the stagecoach being late. Earlier he had conferred with Sheriff Black about the recent telegram telling that Kid LaDuke was last seen at Camas Prairie. Only when the sheriff had told Dancy Stuart that the Kid would strike up into the mountains had he kept from heading out. For up there they'd damnsure need tracker Bonner Hudson.

Further along the street Sheriff Black was gathered with other members of his posse. He took in the rancher and his seven men and Dancy's son, Kelsay. A lot of things were troubling the sheriff at the moment. Kelsay going along was one of them. He was nothing but an irresponsible playboy, and liked to hang out at the bars in Pablo. Then there was the rancher just digging a crude grave for his foreman out at his ranch instead of bringing the body in for a proper burial. Didn't even ask the minister to come out, he mused sadly. About the way you'd treat a dead dog.

Somebody nudged his arm, and Sheriff Harvey Black turned to look at Silas Linderman scanning the southern approaches to town, where the road curled down from a high elevation.

"Couple of riders coming in. So?"

"Back horse is being ridden double."

"Yeah, appears that way," the sheriff pondered as from the opposite way someone called out that the stagecoach was coming in. Like everyone else the sheriff surged in closer to the stage station office, the shout going up that Bonner Hudson was on the stage. "Just gets back, now we're gonna ask him to head out again."

"Think he won't go?"

"Was me, Silas, I'd get my dander up considerable."

Now there were exclamations of surprise, and those in the street were breaking out of the way as the stagecoach picked up speed to roll past the stage station office. It kept on until it cleared the business places on Main Street, where it drew up just as suddenly, Bonner Hudson jumping down by those incoming riders.

While everyone waiting out in the street had their attention focused on the incoming stagecoach, Bonner had been scanning what lay beyond, and even from a distance he'd recognized his wife. He took in the tears suddenly sparkling at the corners of her eyes, and then he was gathering Angelica in his arms and lifting her out of the saddle.

"We came upon her out by the lake, Bonner."

"It was LaDuke, he took Lillian!"

"Your face . . . Lord, honey, what did he do to you . . . ?"

"Oh, guess my arm's broken."

He looked into her eyes with a fierce intensity. "Did, did he touch you?"

"No. Oh, Bonner, I'm afraid for our daughter. There were so many of them . . . and, honey, our house is gone, burned down."

"We can always build another house." He brought her into his arms, and she curled an arm around his neck. Bonner asked the cowhands to tell Doc Waverly to expect another patient. At the moment his concern was so great for his wife that he couldn't build up any anger. That would come later, when he was out on the trail. Coming toward Bonner as he strode quickly down the boardwalk were those who'd been gathered by the stage station office, then Bonner Hudson was swinging onto a side street and angling toward a clinic run by Big Rock's only doctor.

Clustered in the livery stable where Bonner Hudson was saddling his horse were the sheriff and Dancy Stuart. Someone had brought over the gear Bonner had packed along to Idaho, his rifle, and war bag. So far he hadn't said all that much, only that he was heading after the Kid.

Sheriff Harvey Black had hung back to let the rancher have a go with Bonner, and now Bonner looked at Dancy Stuart, and he said coldly, "You'll still pay me five thousand to track down those outlaws. That racehorse must mean a lot to you."

"Now it's your daughter I'm concerned about."

Bonner let that go, his eyes keeping to the task of tightening the saddle cinches. This wasn't the time to judge a man like Dancy Stuart. His mind swung far beyond the stable to the western reaches of the valley, for to judge what Teddy LaDuke would do meant remembering Teddy's personal habits and just what kind of tracker he was. Teddy's heading for the mountains was an indication to Bonner he hadn't really planned this out. As for LaDuke's kidnapping his daughter, it was a ploy to make sure those following him would think twice about using their guns.

"Harv, by now your deputies should be getting close to Camas Prairie."

"I expect they'll pick up the Kid's trail."

"So LaDuke wants forty thousand. Dancy, you'd better withdraw that money out of your bank." Bonner shoved his Winchester into the scabbard, turned back to pick up his war bag, from which he lifted out his gunbelt to strap it around his waist. "Because I don't want my daughter getting killed when we catch up to LaDuke."

Somewhat reluctantly Dancy Stuart said, "I'll do that."

Stowing the contents of his war bag into his saddlebags, Bonner swung into the saddle. "And I'm heading out. I expect you know the way to Camas Prairie. Once I pick up LaDuke's trail, I'll leave markers behind. And Harv, I want to thank you for letting my wife stay at your place." On the way out Bonn Hudson ducked to clear the top of the double doors. Then without glancing at the horsemen assembled out in the street, he reined to cut down a vacant lot and was gone.

Having passed this way before, Bonner Hudson knew it was about fifty miles to Camas Prairie. On the way he bypassed the valley towns and encountered a few on the move same as him, though he rode past without speaking. The set to the tracker's face was language enough. Bonner let go of any thoughts of Angelica or his house, as he absorbed himself completely in the dangerous craft of hunting down lawbreakers.

First of all, there was the track, at best a temporary thing. They dry out and fade. And as they dry, the wind sweeps in to wipe them away. But each trail has an identity all its own. Each has the habitual gait of the person making them; the little nuances in them changed by the flux of emotions as the person Bonner followed moved. But here it would be him picking up hoofmarks made by several horses, something that he knew Kid LaDuke was considering at this very moment. The more Bonner thought on it, the more he was certain that LaDuke would lay ambushes in an attempt to even up the odds.

"The smart thing, Teddy, is for you to clear out alone with the racehorse and leave your men behind to cover your tracks." But that wasn't the Kid's style. As there'd always been others around to share in LaDuke's killing ways.

Bonner was squinting into an afternoon sun

when he rode through Camas Prairie. Quickly he passed through the small cowtown. Ahead lay a series of mountain ranges separated by small valleys and passes leading over them, and no matter which way you headed, just more mountains heaped up. Rivers gorged through them, but not all that many roads, though game trails were plentiful. It would be hard sneaking up on one man, much less a bunch of outlaws. The way tracker Bonner Hudson figured on working it was to keep ahead of Sheriff Black's posse.

It didn't take Bonner all that long to come upon hoofmarks chewing up some bottom ground down by a creek. The spacing between them told him the riders had come through in a hurry. He held there, noticing how water had sucked back into some of the deep hoofprints etched in the soft, loamy soil. He watched as a frog hopped past on its way to the creek. One set of hoofprints he picked out as made by the racehorse, etched how they were shaped to memory. Crossing over, where the ground was harder, he found the markings had more of a discernible shape. Soon he was able to determine which horse his daughter was on, and as he began following the clear trail left by the outlaws, he also saw fresher hoofprints left by horses ridden by Sheriff Black's deputies.

"They're making for the pass between the Cabinets and Flathead mountains. Just hope those deputies have enough sense not to try something." That last thought was caused by worry about Lily, and he kneed his horse into a canter.

With night coming ever closer, Bonner knew those ahead of him would also be seeking a place to make camp. By now it was his opinion that Kid LaDuke was deep into the pass and would wait until morning before breaking out of there. The last town he'd encounter before leaving the valley wasn't all that far to the southwest. His hunch that Jim Bob and the other deputies would be waiting there proved correct when he finally rode in about an hour after the last traces of daylight had vanished. He came in under a tarred sky punched by starlight.

The bronc under him, a mottled gray, had held up well on the long ride over from Big Rock. "A stayer," he remarked as an afterthought as he brought the gray toward one of the few saloons in Perma. Some horses were tied up out front.

"Bonner, you're here?"

Jim Bob Benham, who'd been idling in the open door of the saloon, came out to receive a quiet nod from Bonner Hudson.

"Appears they're headin' into Idaho."

"Appears that way," responded Bonner.

"Well, you're here. So I expect the others aren't that far behind. We could hit into the pass and try for that racehorse; might even get lucky and take out the Kid."

"We can, Jim Bob, but we won't," came the tracker's sharp retort. His glance took in the other deputies coming outside. "They've got my daughter with them."

"Lily?"

Everyone glanced at Rick McPherson.

"Yup, Lily's with them." Bonner didn't feel the need to explain how this had come about. There was a searching gaze at the emotions playing across Rick McPherson's face, which brought Bonner to remembering just how vulnerable young people could be. And too, Rick had been a regular visitor out at his place until Lily had decided it was Kelsay Stuart she wanted to marry. How do you plumb the mind of a woman, especially one you called a daughter?

"Reckon this changes things," said Walt Grisham. "Just can't figure, Bonner, why he kidnapped your daughter."

"She's the Kid's hole card. He knows we're gonna catch up with him. Even then I doubt if he'll let her go . . . even after he trades that racehorse for some of Dancy's money. So, I'll treat you boys to drinks now as I'll be long gone before any of you roll out of the sack."

"No call for you to go on alone."

"Only way I figure I can get Lily back alive. I'll leave sign for you. Be back to drink with you soon's I stable my hoss."

"Bonner, I . . . I'd like to go with you. . . ."

Bonner Hudson turned back. "I appreciate that, Rick. But the cruel hard fact is I don't want you getting me killed. We're not tracking a man up there but some species called sidewinder."

When Bonner had turned to disappear around the side wall of the saloon, he paused to take in the darkening mountains and the lighter patches of snow. For a brief moment he wondered how Angelica was doing. It would be harder on her, as she had to face the possibility of his going under coupled with the awful knowledge Lily might not ever come back too. "Lord, I'm not a prayin' man . . . but I hope you send your angels to watch over my Lily . . . ," he murmured.

Chapter Seven

The shock of seeing Kid LaDuke gun down a man wearing a badge made Lillian Hudson realize the same could happen to her. It had come about so unexpectedly, the town marshal stumbling upon some of the outlaws holding up that dry goods store back at Camas Prairie. The town marshal had been unarmed, and he'd reminded Lillian of the shoemaker back at Big Rock in the way he moved. When he blundered into the store, the Kid's gun had bucked unremorsefully. Then the outlaws had gone about loading up with supplies as if nothing had happened.

The campsite picked by LaDuke was in a serene setting of velvety meadow grass and green-swaying pines. Lillian Hudson sat at the base of a tree, with a rope going around the trunk and tied to her hands; any outlaw daring to get close under the Kid's watchful eyes. Mostly they'd been keeping to the saddle as they'd made that swift ride across the Flathead Valley. Here with the outlaws settling in for the night came this queasy feeling, a mingling of fear and the uncertainties of what LaDuke intended for her. She couldn't shake her mother bringing up what had happened to those two girls over at Lone Tree.

The tension rose in Lillian Hudson whenever she felt Kid LaDuke's eyes sweeping lustfully over her. The rest were just as bad; their snide and ugly remarks had come at her as they rode, and here, the canyon wall seemed to throw back their voices. How could he have changed so much from the Teddy LaDuke she'd known before? Gone so bad, his six-gun an unthinking extension of an evil man, and yet not a man as he was only twenty. But he knew how to use that carrot between his legs, she mused bitterly, as did his companions.

"How's my Lily?"

She swung her head to Kid LaDuke just coming back from tending to his horse. Determined not to show her fear, she kept on staring at him until his smile became a scowl. It came to her in a sudden thought that Teddy LaDuke, despite the gun he carried and the presence of other outlaws, feared her father. The thought comforted her as she watched LaDuke pull a bottle of whiskey out of his saddlebag, the glow of the campfire reflecting in his eyes.

By count there were thirteen of them, an unlucky number, she mused. Came an amusing thought — none of them could probably count that high. Some of them came in, packing bottles or settling their frying pans in the burning wood as it seemed it was every man for himself when it came to chowing down. They were cautious about sharing their whiskey. Beyond under the trees she caught the darker patch of a horse's hide—Daredevil, they called him. Their chatter along the way told of how Dancy Stuart's foreman had been killed. And with an inward sigh Lillian Hudson wondered if Kelsay knew she'd been abducted. She was comforted by the presence of the engagement ring on her left hand, which she'd worked around so the small diamond didn't show. But now for some strange reason another face came to mind, with Lillian murmuring silently, "Rick McPherson . . . haven't seen him lately." But why think about Rick now as she was absolutely certain it was Kelsay she loved.

"Hey, Kid," said Inky Braxton as he settled down Indian-fashion a short distance from the large campfire. "How much longer you figure on keeping this up?"

"We'll keep to the mountains until we find out how many are after us."

"Yeah, I'll buy that."

Guardedly the Kid swung his eyes around to check on what the others were doing. He refrained from saying anything as the others crowded in around the campfire. He caught Wiley Sheldon's eye as he leaned in closer to Braxton to whisper, "Let's take a walk."

That ambling walk brought the three of them back up to their horses, where they stood watching the racehorse. They turned so each of them could watch in different directions, a habit of men on the dodge. "Forty thousand split thirteen ways doesn't come out to a hell of a lot."

"You been reading my mind, Kid?"

He grinned at the mulatto.

Wiley Sheldon said, "Speaking of splitting up that money, just want to mention I overheard Cunny and Walker and Cowgar jawing away."

"Cunny—a troublesome bastard. He could just get it in his head to take me out. Trouble is, he can't find his way out of a whorehouse without help. So, if he wants gunplay I'll oblige him. But not the way he expects."

"Is this another devious notion, Kid?"

Kid LaDuke's laughter spilled toward the horses. Then the young woman they held captive cut loose with a high-pitched scream. The horses surged away from the picket line, bucking and whickering, with some of them breaking away, and the Kid yelling, "Tend to the hosses."

Kid LaDuke spun around and ran toward the campfire. He tripped over something but managed to regain his balance, and when he broke in under screening trees, as yet not having unleathered his six-gun, he saw that it was Cal Walker sprawled down by the girl, the others taking this in from the fringes of the fire. The hardcase had one hand inside Lillian Hudson's blouse and an arm encircling her waist, and there was a broad grin on his bearded face.

"Damn, you smell good. That's it . . . cuss me out, gal . . ."

"Walker! You unsorry bastard!" Palming his six-gun, the Kid felt it buck in his hand, and what Cal Walker felt was a slug penetrating into the upper part of his skull. He wore no hat and the top of his head seemed to burst away like a melon being ripped open, and blood and white brain matter splashed onto Lily Hudson as the hardcase sagged down dead. Anticipatory smiles were ripped away as the Kid pulled out his other six-gun. "Well?"

The wrath of Kid LaDuke was something they'd seen unleashed before.

"Some of the hosses broke away. Get out there and help round them up."

"Damn."

That single comment took them into the shadows, all except for Cunny, who said, "You didn't have to kill Walker. He was just havin' a little fun."

"He crossed the line, and you know that. Since you two seemed to be buddying up to one another, maybe you can have the pleasure of dragging his body out of here."

"I'll do that, Kid," said Cunny, "but I still say you were too damned hasty."

With the body being pulled away, the Kid could see how Lily Hudson's blouse had been torn, and he leathered his guns before shrugging out of his coat. "I told them not to bother you."

"Why don't you just let me go?"

"I do that and they'll turn on me like a pack of wolves."

"They're worse than any animal. And so are you. You come in . . . burn our house down . . . beat up my mother . . ."

"Had to do it. Your ma has got a mean mouth,

72

never did cotton to me." He untied her hands, and watched as she donned his leather coat; then he re-tied the rope. "Get what sleep you can as we'll be pulling out long before first light."

"Where are we going?"

"There's a heap of mountains out here." Un-crouching, he waved a vague hand.

"Hudson'll track you vermin down."

Just for a second his eyes grew ugly, and he considered finishing what Cal Walker had started. What had happened at Lone Tree came to mind, those two girls being raped, the pleasure afterward of taking a knife to them. The tip of his boot lashed out so suddenly there wasn't even a blink of surprise from Lily Hudson. The boot caught her near the right temple to render her unconscious.

"About the only way to shut a woman up."

Strung out in a ragged line on the stageline road wending out of the canyon, the outlaws were confronted with the choice of continuing on to the town of Paradise or forking their horses southwesterly. It was still dark enough so that the cold of night hadn't lifted, and they all wore yellow slickers. Humped all around them were dark mountains. The sky grayed, and here and there were a few stars.

The racehorse, Daredevil, had grown accustomed to being led now by a single horseman. The Kid had insisted they take along Cal Walker's horse, with the saddle still cinched to it. The Kid rode up front holding on to the reins of Lily Hudson's

73

bronc. Every so often Lily's eyes would bore into the Kid's back. Gone was her fear of last night over that outlaw trying to have his way with her. Her head still ached from where Kid LaDuke had kicked her, this cowardly blow more than anything having given Lily the determination to resist. She'd pieced together the Kid's reasons for taking her along.

Now Kid LaDuke called out they'd be heading southwesterly around Big Hole Peak. "Some of us will," he went on. "We'll split up. As we've got to find out how many are behind us."

"Plenty of high rocks around here to set up an ambush."

"I know, Cunny, but we just could kill Dancy Stuart."

"The rancher. What if he didn't bring any money along?"

"Dancy's a greedy sonofabitch. He'll be comin' after us awright. But with a lot of men backin' him up. What he figures to happen is gettin' his hoss back without havin' to fork over that money. That's all changed now that we've got Bonner's daughter."

"How'd you figure that, Kid?"

"If Dancy tries holdin' out so that Bonner's kid here gets hurt, Bonner'll kill Dancy—pure and simple."

"Maybe so."

"No maybe about it."

To the beating of wings a night hawk barely cleared the horsemen clustered in a loose circle, and some glanced skyward to realize easterly pink traceries of light had appeared. These were men more favoring the night, as daybreak would see them saddlebound and maybe running into some lawmen.

"I expect Bonner Hudson won't be misled by this, that he'll come after me. Bonner'll be way ahead of the others. Just let him come on."

Kid LaDuke and five other hardcases held there as the others followed the wider sweepings of a canyon passing to the northwest. With them went Wiley Sheldon, to more or less keep control of things. From what he knew of rancher Dancy Stuart, the Kid figured Dancy might not want to be part of Sheriff Harvey Black's posse. If that posse came in first, there was an order passed along by Kid LaDuke for his men to open fire.

"This'll damnsure cause a lot of them to suddenly decide to skedaddle back where they came from. Even the odds up considerable."

"I figure it will, Kid," threw in Inky Braxton. "One thing, if this tracker is out front, Cunny might decide he's fair game."

"That's why I put Wiley in charge. Well, Lily, time to head out. Them ropes too tight?"

"I can manage," she replied bitterly.

"Maybe I should have let that hardcase get to you," he snapped back "Awright, let's hit the trail."

Chapter Eight

Late that afternoon Hudson Bonner took in the debris of empty whiskey bottles and food scrapings left behind by the outlaws. What had drawn him away from the trail were encircling turkey vultures and his fear that he would find the body of his daughter. Instead there'd been the remains of an outlaw, the body being clawed and pecked apart just downslope from where he stood. Out of a sense of decency he had placed stones over the body, even as he tried to piece together what had happened.

Spiraling upward near the barren road were little dust eddies caused by the wind picking up. He could feel the power contained in the mountainous updraft of hot summery wind. About midway up the mountain he could make out some vultures just seeming to perch up there on outstretched wings, probably perturbed over this intrusion. He knew from the thick silence that the Kid and his murdering chums were long gone. He said, "One down and twelve to go."

As he'd ridden in, Bonner had taken the time to loosen saddle cinches and adjust the bridle, as it seemed to be chaffing the horses's mouth. There was a deliberateness to the way he moved, a slowness deceiving to men unused to the ways of a tracker. As to where Bonner Hudson was—in the western extremities of this passageway through these mountains—he knew he was the only critter in it accustomed to walking on its hind legs. They—Kid LaDuke's gang—would be on theirs as they rode sizing up a place to make camp.

"Hope they make one helluva fire."

He walked his horse out from under the trees, the vague stench of rotting flesh a remindful annoyance, and then went back to the stagecoach road. He'd pulled out of Perma just as the last stragglers were heading out of the saloons, a scanty two hours after he sacked in. Bellies bloated out with hard liquor, they probably hadn't noticed the passage of the tracker.

There was some concern when Bonner's horse brought him to hoofmarks telling of the outlaws pulling up to mill their horses about. He could almost picture it, his eyes taking in the marks left by Dancy's racehorse, those of the horse ridden by Lily, a scant yard away the dust-implanted ironshod prints of the bronc ridden by Teddy LaDuke. Here he found the outlaws had split into two bunches, with Bonner barely letting his horse lose stride as he veered it southwesterly. From here on the spacings told Bonner those he were tracking were reining their horses out more. But he held his mount to a lope, jutting ahead of him to separate one canyon from another, the rising sweep of a mountain still a considerable distance away. The day shadows danced away more from the screening trees. Tonight, Bonner figured, he should come in on them. Along with this grim thought: if Teddy'd harmed Lily same's he'd done to her mother he'd never see another sunrise.

Standard regalia for men on the dodge were field glasses, with both Wiley Sheldon and hard-case Cunny taking in the lonely horseman. They knew roughly from directions given to them by Kid LaDuke that a few miles deeper into this mountain valley lay the town of Paradise. That if they kept heading in to hook up with the rest of the gang they'd have to pass along the entire length of the Cabinets, roughly a distance just under a hundred miles, and then cut southerly.

"The way this hombre rides he ain't ajust headin' into Paradise to buy a sack of flour."

"You figure it's that tracker—"

About Cunny was an air of cold disdain as he glanced over at Wiley Sheldon squatting down on a flat rock. Up here on a rocky elevation they had a commanding view of the canyon where they'd spent the night. His full name Travis Boyd Cunny, he was the product of a Galveston whore and some drifting cowhand. He'd been orphaned when he was barely out of his diapers. All he'd known was hardship, so it seemed perfectly natural him being a lawbreaker. He had a tendency to get sun blisters on his face, so he wore a wide-brimmed Stetson tucked low over his forehead. Another natural move was him parding up with Spade Cowgar, whose last place of honest employment had been down in the Panhandle. The deeper he got into these mountains, the more Cunny realized it was a bad move leaving the openness of country further south. On the way up they'd passed a lot of tinderbox banks. What struck him the most was the look of prosperity in the Flathead Valley. If this racehorse deal didn't pan out that's where he meant to head.

He turned his head ever so slightly to whisper to Cowgar, "Still out of rifle range."

"You decide to take that rider out, I'll back your play. Some of the others are gettin' tired of how the Kid's been ramroddin' this thing."

In the distant haze they took in Bonner Hudson angling to the south, and with Cunny sighting in through his eyeglass eastward along the canyon floor. Lowering the glasses, he eased back to get under a ledge and out from under sunlight. It would take the rider he'd seen another good half hour to get within range. He hand-rolled a cigarette and got to musing that the Kid could be right about that rancher and some lawmen coming after them — but where the hell were they?

The ledge they were on had an access route to the north, and it was part of the lower reaches of a mountain. He heard the low rumble of thunder and gazed northeasterly at one big black thunderhead trying to shoulder in against a mountain, with the wind currents around the high rocky mass starting to break up the cloud. The call, "Some more riders," brought Cunny out to join his companions.

"Three of them," Wiley Sheldon went on.

"Some posse," blustered Cowgar, a man with no distinguishing features except for the scar that had split his upper lip.

"One's holding back. Went in under some trees." Wiley Sheldon swung his glasses to a pair of riders taking the northern road that would carry them to Paradise. "Maybe some advance riders."

"What about that first one we've seen?"

"Damn, he was there a moment ago?"

Birds were the watchdogs of the mountain forest, and it was the birds that tipped Bonner Hudson to the presence of the outlaws. Distantly he'd heard their chattering up near where the mountain began, and now he could hear some lifting up from the trees that clung to the rocky slopes. So where the trail had dipped into a hollow, he'd simply held there. The trail higher ahead shielded him from those he'd been tracking. Behind and lower he could see where the trail came out of the canyon. Like the outlaws Bonner had a field glass, and through it he took in Deputy Sheriffs McPherson and Jim Bob Benham just starting to bring their horses onto the stagecoach road forking off to the north. Another piece of gear Bonner had packed along was a mirror small enough to fit into his shirt pocket.

Among other things last night he'd told the deputies that if possible he would send back a mirrored signal if he spotted danger ahead, and now he held it so that it caught the rays of the sun to reflect them back toward the canyon. By flicking his wrist he semaphored a message back to the deputies. He wasn't sure if they'd picked it up, but he muttered, "They know what to expect out here."

Repocketing the mirror, Bonner found a spot near some brush where he had a commanding view of the mountain. It wasn't as high here as further westward, but it still served as a formidable barrier. He knew it wouldn't be the Kid up there, but some the Kid had left behind to harry their pursuers. Where the Kid was heading, a narrow valley that would eventually take him up through Lookout Pass, there were some water holes, and before that, some small settlements. There was also a river, the St. Regis. But once the Kid got up into the pass, anybody behind him would come under the Kid's guns. The pass was part of the Bitterroots, a larger mountain range beyond which lay Idaho. Or those outlaws could strike to the southeast this side of the Bitterroots and head down toward Missoula.

"Sooner or later Teddy LaDuke has to make a stand. But at a place where he holds all the cards. Lily . . . just hope you're okay . . ."

The glare of the signal mirror as caught by Rick McPherson sent him shouldering his horse into

Benham's. It broke the cantering stride of both horses, and then they were skirting away from the road to find shelter. "You know this country better'n me."

"Not like Bonner does." Jim Bob Benham reached around for his canteen and at the same time lifted his gaze to the mountain off to the southwest. "Plenty of places to sit up there and view anybody coming out of that canyon. But with approaches from both sides I think it's some men left behind by LaDuke. Probably to find out what he's up against."

Though screened from the eyes of the outlaws, they could still study the other fork of the road taken by Bonner Hudson, and saw that it ran along more open ground. Where they were, amongst some massive boulders and scrub brush, they could make out just to the north of them a draw working its way along the valley floor, the road more or less following along it.

"That posse shouldn't be all that far behind us, Jim Bob."

"Right now Bonner's my concern. If he keeps heading along that other road they're sure to pick him off. What we need is a diversion."

"Yeah, work our way along that draw. Then pull out of it and head in toward the mountain; lots of cover south of the road too. We might not get any of them, but at least it'll give Bonner a chance to get through."

Up on the rocky ledge Cowgar blurted out, "Just what the hell's goin' on—"

Wiley Sheldon replied, "Easy to figure out. See those birds hopping out of those trees down below. Warned them."

"What do you think?"

Wiley swatted at a mosquito as he turned his attention to Cunny pulling his rifle out of the saddle sheath. Their horses were tethered lower on the long ledge, around to the north where there was more shade. He waddled back, his mouth tugged down in a displeased grimace.

"What I think is that I'm gettin' damned sick of crawlin' around these mountains. They've picked up on where we pulled apart. The first one we saw used a mirror to flash back a message. Just three of them. All this talk of the Kid's about some posse. I say we catch up to the others."

"Hey! There he goes!"

Breaking into the open trail came Bonner Hudson, crouched to the far side of his saddle. He caught the glint of sunlight on a rifle barrel, and when the rifle sounded, the slug from it plowed into the ground far behind the legs of his galloping horse. More rifles opened up, and for Bonner there came some anxious moments. He wondered if those deputies would back his trying to get through. His answer came a moment later as the gunfire from above tapered off, to open up again to the north.

"It's those last two we saw!"

"Where the hell are they?" screamed Cowgar as a slug struck rock near his head to fling needle-sharp chips at his face.

As he moved to get a better firing position, one of the outlaws took a slug directly in the center of his chest. He fell forward to follow the plunge of his rifle down a hundred feet or more to waiting rocks.

Now something to the east caught Wiley Sheldon's eye, and from where he lay, bellydown, he stopped firing and shouted, "Look at them! Got to be forty or more!"

Pulling back from the edge of the ledge, the outlaws took in the expected appearance of the posse, which, though, still in the mouth of the canyon, was pouring down the stagecoach road in response to the distant reverberating of gunfire. They all broke for their horses. They followed Cunny's flight down the more hazardous way to the south. As they descended, their horses dropped back on their haunches, as they descended pitching down gravel and pebbly rocks and kicking up dust. They reclaimed the trail taken by Kid La-Duke and reined their horses out for about a mile before easing them into a canter.

"The Kid was right."

"How many did you count?"

Wiley Sheldon said, "Too damned many. And don't forget there's one ahead of us."

"Yeah, that damned tracker, Bonner Hudson."

But the unexpected booming of the tracker's rifle proved them wrong, as Cowgar and another hardcase pitched out of their saddles. The shots came from behind and off to the southeast, and the rest of the outlaws spurred their broncs into a frightened gallop westerly along the trail.

A grim smile etched on his face, Bonner said, "Don't know if they left any behind back there. But there's two more we won't have to fret about."

Chapter Nine

Overnighting at Camas Prairie hadn't been Sheriff Harvey Black's idea. In the bars the members of his posse found out how the town marshal had been gunned down, and it didn't take some of them too long to change their minds about going on. But when they pulled out the following morning there were still a lot of them.

Now it was with a sense of relief that Sheriff Black returned Walt Grisham's short nod of greeting, and Grisham went on to say that the other deputies had gone on ahead. "Just up there is where they camped; left a dead man behind."

"Well, Harv, what are we waiting for?" Dancy Stuart kept walking his horse in closer, and a couple of riders had to wheel their horses aside. He hadn't wanted to hook up with the posse, as he had brought along eleven men. He was still rankling over the way Bonner Hudson had practically ordered him to pack along that forty thousand.

86

"For one thing, Dancy," the sheriff said just as harshly, "to hear my deputy out."

Walt Grisham simply ignored the rancher as he kept his eyes on the man he worked for. "Bonner must have pulled out long before we even thought of getting up, Harv," he said. "Just up ahead we found where they split up. Danny and Jim Bob went on to scout out how many are headed for Paradise. Didn't leave all that long . . ."

It was at that moment that the outlaws opened up on Bonner Hudson. The sheriff and his deputy were the first to break through the scattering of horsemen. They were still in the canyon but pounding down the lowering track of the stage-coach road, and only when they cleared the canyon did the sheriff out front rein up sharply as he reached the fork in the main road. Reining his horse around in a tight circle, he barked orders, not giving a damn if he was usurping the authority Dancy Stuart felt he had out here. As a result, the riders scattered to either side, Sheriff Black going with the southern bunch. He wasn't aware until later that Dancy Stuart had gone the other way; what held his eyes and attention to the west were the muzzle blasts of weaponry.

Just as quickly, the fire tapered off, with Sheriff Black and those with him still about four miles away from the rising hulk of the mountain, but a few hillocks in between and some trees.

"Some riders are coming down! Not all that many, maybe five of them!"

"Maybe the Kid?"

The sheriff yelled back, "Not his style to take any chances." When the riders disappeared behind some rocks, he slowed his horse down. Out here he figured it to be a long haul, and he didn't want to be setting on a tired horse. Now in looking around he noticed some of Dancy's men were along, and his deputy, Walt Grisham. "At least they aren't all that far ahead."

"They'd of been long gone," spoke up a cowhand named Ray Jarvis, "if the Kid hadn't detoured way over there to kidnap Bonner's daughter. Wonder how Bonner's feeling about now?"

"Wonder where the heck he's at right now," countered the sheriff. He followed after Grisham, striking away from the trail and northward along the lower land comprising the valley floor.

They veered westerly upon sighting the rest of the posse sitting their horses by an upheaval of mountainous rocks. A few had dismounted and were working upward behind Danny McPherson, and when the sheriff got there, he learned one of the outlaws had been killed. One of those with McPherson was Dancy Stuart taking in the body sprawled awkwardly in a jumbling of rocks. "Too bad it isn't the Kid."

"Do we just leave him there?"

The rancher didn't bother looking at deputy McPherson as he said cuttingly, "That's what he would do to you." His turning away brought everyone after him.

While the men who'd gone up to view the body were reclaiming their horses, Sheriff Black took stock of the present situation. There were less than fifteen of them now, and he'd divined Kid La-Duke's intentions of keeping on the move until he was deeper in the mountains. It wasn't just a case of trying to overtake the outlaws now that the Kid had Bonner's daughter. His fear was that if they caught up to those outlaws, LaDuke would use Lily Hudson as a human shield; the Kid was mean enough to pull something like that. The key, of course, was Dancy's money. Funny, but the talk of both Dancy and his son had been all about that racehorse.

He reined his horse some so that he could take in Kelsay Stuart swiping at his mouth after drinking from his canteen. Kelsay had been chumming up to one of the younger cowhands and Carl Hanna, a stock clerk at a local dry goods store. The three of them had been hanging back as they rode, cracking jokes and seemingly unconcerned about what lay ahead. It had gotten to Harvey Black, firmed up his belief that Kelsay wasn't in love with Lily Hudson; he just wanted to possess her because Lily was so goldang pretty. That smile creasing across Kelsay Stuart's face would sure enough disappear if Bonner suddenly rode in. And easing his horse over now was Jim Bob Benham, to have a quiet word with the sheriff.

"We laid down screening fire for Bonner Hudson. If he got through, he's between those who went ahead and the ones we fired at."

"Appears they didn't go through Paradise but southerly. How's McPherson doing?"

"Like Rick was born to be a star-packer. We were both cutting loose with our longguns, so there's some question as to which one of us killed that hardcase lying dead yonder. But between us, Harv, it was Rick."

"The first man he's ever shot at, much less killed. Let's bury that between us, Walt."

"Sometimes it's better a man don't know."

"Okay, okay," Dancy Stuart called out, "we won't catch up to those outlaws this way." He didn't wait as some began climbing into their saddles; he reined out with all of his Double S waddies flanking behind, as did Kelsay Stuart and Carl Hanna, who bounced on the saddle as he tried to keep up.

Hanna, Sheriff Black mused, would be one of the first to drop out. Others had already dropped out back at Camas Prairie, as he'd expected from men unused to packing guns, much less going after so dangerous a man as Kid LaDuke. What he feared along the way was the Kid setting up an ambush. But there was Bonner Hudson to warn them—that is if Bonner was still alive.

When they cleared the eastern reaches of the mountain and were in between the mountain and another just to the south, they came upon the rancher and his men, who were bunched up, viewing the two men gunned down by Bonner Hudson. Distantly one of their horses could be seen taking a wary look at the rest of the posses coming up. When they rode on, Sheriff Black was alongside the rancher.

"Get this straight, Dancy, that was a damnfool thing to do back there."

"Your opinion, Harv, never carried much weight with me. I'm here to try and save a very valuable piece of property. Dammit, I paid a heap for Daredevil."

"What about Lily? You've never mentioned her once."

"She's important too."

As he pulled back a little, Sheriff Harvey Black felt revulsion. The naked inflection in the rancher's voice had been one of cold disinterest; clearly Dancy's only concern was for his horse. Through eyes gone flinty the sheriff took in a low line of clouds moving in to the western sky. The rain would be to the Kid's advantage.

First Grisham, then Rick McPherson, spurred up to come in on either side of the sheriff, their horses moving at a fast canter through still another valley. The trail was fairly level. Grass grew between its two ruts, which were hardpanned so that most of the horsemen could keep pace with the leaders out among the prairie grass and sagebrush and old cow chips. The scent of rain had reached them from the clouds darkening to the southwest. The distant flashes of lightning worried them all.

"St. Regis, over the next couple of rises, I'm hoping."

"Reckon we can wait out this storm there as the rain'll wipe out any tracks. It'll be tough goin' for them too."

91

Rick McPherson tugged his hat lower and said quietly, "I just hope Lily's all right, that . . ."

"If she's anything like her pa she'll weather this out."

"Yeah, Bonner, he killed those two back there," murmured the sheriff. "Spooked the rest after the Kid. But rain or no, Bonner'll track 'em down."

Chapter Ten

It turned out to be one of those rainstorms that lingered on for a couple of days. During its passing, creeks born up in the Bitterroots became swollen cataracts which sent cold rainwater into the St. Regis River, eventually overrunning its banks. The storm caused rockslides and avalanches, and Bonner Hudson knew that a lot of livestock had perished and maybe a cowhand or two.

There came a low rumbling sound to Bonner as he saddled his horse in the musky quietness of a pole barn. Backtracking to where he'd gunned down those hardcases, Bonner had kept after the others, holding back some, as he wanted them to hook up with Kid LaDuke. They'd kept right on through St. Regis on the gravel road that centered the narrow valley. Sometime later, the storm struck with a vengeance, a vicious downpouring of rain and hail backed by sudden gusts of wind. There'd been sheet lightning brilliantly etching the Bitterroots angling away to the southeast. Then just about total darkness; Bonner Hudson was barely able to see more'n forty rods in any direction, and the same held true for those he was following.

Without realizing it, he'd drifted away from the road, and it was about here that he struck onto a line fence, which he rode along, at the same time worrying that if the lightning didn't char him out of the saddle falling rocks would do the chore. The fence hooked onto a gate, beyond which a cluster of buildings huddled in a narrow canyon. He rode on in, to be given shelter by the owner of this small spread and his wife and small brood of children. Though he took his meals in the log cabin, it was in the pole barn where he'd bedded down, and now was on the verge of leaving.

"Obliged for your hospitality, Mr. Jessen. I've got a place up in the mountains too. Worry sometimes about being buried under rocks."

"That one was deeper in the canyon. I reckon it's providence that determines our fate, Mr. Hudson. I'd sure like to help you look for your daughter."

"I don't want your children worrying about their pa. You've been most kind." He led his horse out into light drizzling rain. It was lighter out this morning, with the clouds starting to disperse, and cool and just about right for a long ride.

"Careful on that road as there'll be a lot of places washed out. God go with you, Mr. Bonner."

Bonner's casual smile brought him away from the pole barn and past the log cabin, where he duffed his Stetson to wave it at the rancher's children crowding the open back door, and at the woman just back of them, her eyes brimming with concern for Bonner Hudson.

In the barren yard, the claybank's hoofs made a sucking noise each time one of them pulled free of the mud. Then it was loping over rain-glistening meadow grass. He came out of the canyon, and once Bonner was past the line fence, his angling course brought him to the northwest. He'd set his mind to the fact the storm had changed everything. He had a sudden thought that during it Kid La-Duke could have doubled back through the valley and headed back to the Flathead or passed south-easterly along the Bitterroots.

"Nope, there's too much at risk for him. He can't take a chance of getting Dancy's racehorse crippled up. Teddy'll want to have control of things. A place where nobody can sneak up on him. Which has got to be up in Lookout Pass."

Though the cooler weather had made the clay-bank eager to set a faster gait, Bonner kept it loping, even on the gravel road, where in places potholes were full of water. His first anxious moment came when he reached a place where the road dipped into what before had been a creek about barren of water. Now mud-colored creek water roiled angrily downslope. A section of road had been gouged away, but the creek didn't seem all that deep, and he decided to cross. Circling around and away from the creek, he patted the claybank's shoulder before spurring it into a canter and out into the swirling waters. The current carried Bonner past the limits of the road before his horse touched bottom and struggled up onto the far bank. Here he dismounted to check his saddle rigging and let the horse settle down and shake some of the water away. When Bonner rode on, it was a worry of his having to cross the river that the rancher had told him lay ahead.

Further along, on an elevation, he took the time to look back through his field glass in the hopes he might scope in on Sheriff Black and his posse. All he sighted were shafts of sunlight piercing through the clouds, and he rode on, a man alone and filled with concern for his daughter.

Never before had Salt Creek seen the likes of men such as Kid LaDuke and his gang of high riders. It was the last outpost before the road started up the mountainside to plunge through Lookout Pass. For starters the faded sign one saw just before entering Salt Creek had lying figures on it, as it listed the population at twenty-three, when in fact two more families had moved out this past summer. A few empty buildings lay along the main drag, which was merely a wider spot in the road. The rainstorm had laid siege to Salt Creek, as had the outlaws holed up in the Lookout Saloon. But where the downpour had only caused a few roofs to leak and generally chewed up the street outside, these outlaws had brought in fear, not so much that someone living here would get gunned down, but of how they'd been treating the women.

The trouble had started about an hour after the outlaws had ridden in, and just about when the rainstorm hit. Coming out to greet the men pulling up to his livery stable had been Otis Kincaid. Kincaid wore a hook to replace an arm lost while serving as a cavalryman in the Indian Wars, and he was a stubby man in his fifties. He appreciated fine horseflesh, and the racehorse caught his eye. He couldn't help noticing the way one of the outlaws had yanked the woman off her horse. Just about then a woman widowed the past summer, when her cowboy husband had been killed in a ranch accident, chanced to saunter by and go into the Lookout Saloon. It was just Hazel Enright going in for her customary afternoon drink.

"Not all that bad," Inky Braxton had commented.

The other outlaws agreed as they set about stabling their horses. The hostler judged them to be just some hardcases passing through. He guessed rightly that the coming storm was holding them up.

Later on Otis Kincaid was to say ruefully that he wished a couple of other women hadn't passed by just as the outlaws were emerging from his livery stable. But they had, and they were Connie Watson and her daughter, Karen, who was just about the same age as the woman riding with these hardcases. They were going upstreet to the store run by Connie's husband, where everyone bought their groceries and picked up their mail if it chanced to come in that week.

Before riding in, Kid LaDuke had untied the ropes binding Lily's hands, though he still held on to the reins of her horse, with a warning that she keep her mouth shut. Once he'd set his eyes on Salt Creek he knew it wouldn't have any law. Here they could wait for the others to catch up. And there was a smile for the clouds sweeping in over the higher mountains westerly.

97

"Your old man is gonna get soaked."

"He'll find you."

"Oh, I know that, Lily gal. But you mouth off or try anything stupid . . ."

The only ones holding sway in the Lookout Saloon that evening were the outlaws and Hazel Enright. There was an older woman serving as barmaid, but she slipped out the back door when a couple of her customers spoke of going for their guns.

"Dammit, Higgins, I don't want you and Petrie using them guns!"

"Kid, you tell Petrie that as I'm damn well primed to oblige him." In rising, the outlaw had knocked his chair over, and he reached back to tip it upright while glaring across the table.

LaDuke had made arrangements for everyone to sleep in the rooms above the bar. And he felt good about making it this far. Wedged in a chair by his table sat Lily Hudson, as yet not touching the glass of beer the Kid had shoved before her. The bruise at her forehead was purple ugly, with her once in a while receiving wondering glances from the barkeep. A half-hearted poker game was in progress, but everyone seemed more inclined to keep drinking. There was no piano, but someone had left a banjo on which Inky Braxton was plunking out a tune.

As the night progressed, the storm came in more to hammer a murmuring song upon the saloon. The talk in the place centered around the table where Hazel Enright was holding court. She didn't seem perturbed to find they were hardcases as they kept

98

on buying drinks, their eyes going from her to Lily Hudson.

"Who were those other women we saw going into that store . . ."

"There aren't too many women in Salt Creek; must have been the storekeeper's missus." Hazel Enright's cowman's hat was pressed over silky light brown hair, and she had on a plaid coat, under that a cotton shirt and Levi's hanging over high-heeled boots. She was a full-bodied woman whose past social life included evenings spent in bars such as this with her late husband, and her conversation included a few choice words that pleased her table companions. She didn't have any hankering to head out with them, as one of the hardcases had been so bold to ask. But the loneliness of living in a place such as Salt Creek held her here.

"That store's still open."

The Kid cast an idle glance at Petrie going to stand by the open batwings after his encounter with the other hardcase. "Bardog, this metropolis got a café?"

"I can rustle you up some cold grub, cold cuts, the like." Despite all the cuss words being tossed about, bartender Elroy Hattan had responded with a few polite nods and a smile. He didn't want to get drawn into anything. Though up until a half hour ago there'd been coins chinking onto his bar, now they merely called out, demanding a cold glass of beer or bottle of whiskey, without bothering to pay. It was going to be a long night, and if this rain kept up they just might hold in here only hell knew how long.

"I see one of them women," Petrie said loudly. "Think I'll just head over there and see if I can buy her a drink or two."

"There was the pair of them?"

"Yup, the other one's still there."

This prompted two other hardcases to trail after Petrie, who was striding outside despite the rain flailing around the saloon so hard that water was starting to run in the wide space of road between the buildings. The Kid shouted after them to bring back some vittles. This was followed by a thunderclap so loud it seemed to rattle windowpanes in the Lookout Saloon, while serving to spur those outside into a high-stepping run to get out of the rain.

Petrie caught the front door as it swung open. He had a smile for the surprised look in the woman's face, and she stammered, "Sorry, we're just closing up."

"You don't say," he retorted as she began backing away from the outlaw. He took in her flaxen hair and the curving sweep of her shoulders under the shawl.

"Now look here," blustered the storekeeper.

The other outlaws shoving in held back the storekeeper's words. Aaron Watson was a big man gone soft. He resented the way they were looking at his wife and daughter. He'd seen them ride in and was hoping they were something other than men on the dodge, as through Salt Creek came a lot of men in a hurry to get over Lookout Pass and into the deeper spread of mountains beyond. "Well, if it's groceries you want—"

One of the hardcases, a Kansan named Chandler,

cast an appreciative eye at some smoked hams and sausages hanging from wall hooks back of a counter. He picked at his nose around a grin that split his thick lips to show gaps between his teeth. Stepping closer to the counter, he took in the old cash register.

"Now, look here, mister . . ."

With a casual movement of his hand, Chandler pulled out his Navy Colt, and just as casually said, "Those gunnysacks back there; pack those hams and sausages in 'em, and I like the looks of those apples."

"You want one of 'em?"

Chandler shot a glance at the women. "Maybe the storekeeper has something to say about that. She your wife?"

"My wife and daughter. Look, take the meat and just leave us alone."

Until now Petrie had been content to let Chandler hog the show, but now he reached out a gloved hand to touch the woman's hair. Connie Watson pulled away. "Ma'am, I came over to ask if you wanted to come over to the saloon for a few drinks. You're an awful wholesome woman in that yellow dress. Same goes for your daughter."

"No, I, please, I beg you to just go away."

"Chandler, watta you think?"

"I want those hams and what's in that money box. Take the women if you've a mind to." His words brought the storekeeper breaking around the counter. Chandler wheeled that way and snapped off a quick shot, the bullet gouging across the

101

countertop. "The next one'll part your hair."

"Ladies, if you please." Around a lustful grin Petrie and the other hardcase eased both women out through the open door. "You gals behave and nothing'll happen to your husband."

"What's your name, gal?"

"Kar . . . Karen . . ."

"Mine's Steve Beaudine. Here now, pull that shawl over your head so's not to get your hair all wet in this rain."

Inside the store, Chandler kept his gun trained on Aaron Watson, who was barely able to restrain himself, his big hands working and trembling as he considered reaching for one of the handguns he kept as part of his merchandise. The outlaw motioned for the storekeeper to pick up one of the gunnysacks that were piled by some barrels. Teasingly Chandler muttered, "Awful hard on a man seeing his women going out with someone else. Just maybe they'll have a better time than being out with a sourpuss like you." Doubling his fist, he brought it down on the cash register keys, to have the drawer spring open.

"Damn . . . you . . ."

All the hardcase did in response was to laugh as he emptied the drawer of what money it contained. Under different circumstances such an outburst would have brought him to killing the storekeeper. But thinking of the mental torture the man must feel seeing his women abused like this was more enjoyable to the hardcase. When Chandler left, it was after he'd emptied the handguns he found behind the counter and tossed them out into the rainsogged street, then he followed hefting two gunny-sacks.

Crossing over, he muttered, "If that storekeeper has any balls he'll be comin' after his women — be a pleasure killing the stingy sonofabitch."

The sight of women she knew being forced into the saloon had brought forcibly home to Hazel Enright the cruel nature of these men. Where before she'd been holding her own in bantering talk, it came clear to her with an inward queasiness that these men meant to have more than just her sharing some drinks. Calmly, came an inner voice, as she watched the one known as Petrie force Connie Watson onto a chair at one of the tables, and then to have Connie's daughter scoot onto another chair.

"Well, ladies," boomed Kid LaDuke, "welcome to our little party. He kicked out at Lily Hudson's chair. "This here gal is Lily. But with that sour face she ain't no lily of the valley. Me, I'm Kid LaDuke. You, bardog, I don't see you comin' over to ask what the ladies want. Hop to it, dammit." His words had gotten slurry, but he felt good. He was in out of the weather and he expected to come into a lot of money. There was also the way he'd gotten to snake glances at Bonner's daughter slumped to his right. Once when he was a lot younger he'd chanced to come across Lily naked and just about to take a plunge into the creek running by their place. She'd filled out a lot more since then. The Kid's fear of Bonner Hudson dimmed as his eyes caressed Lily.

103

* * *

What was different about the St. Regis was its being the only eastward-flowing river west of the Continental Divide, a sobering fact Bonner Hudson discovered long after night had settled upon the valley. His view of the river was from the east bank. There was enough starlight to show where the bridge had been washed away, with his horse nervously prancing away from the sound of the rushing waters.

Further study told Bonner the river wasn't as high, but even so he couldn't risk crossing here. Perhaps by morning he could find a place to cross further upriver. The outlaws he'd been tracking must have gotten through before the bridge was gone, or else like he'd be doing tonight, they were out setting up a campsite.

He walked his horse off the road and held it to an easy walk as he followed the river wending toward the blacker hulk of the Bitterroots. Cottonwoods fringed upon the river, and when he scared up some deer, it came to him that the St. Regis was a tributary of the bigger Bitterroot River and that he should be coming to where the rivers enjoined. In the settling fabric of night he realized that to go on was just begging for trouble.

"Can't shake the feeling, though, that the Kid isn't all that far away." His eyes kept piercing toward the river, which glinted wetly, still swollen to the tops of its high banks. He knew about undercurrents in western rivers. Once he'd almost drowned in an attempt to cross the Snake River on a night such as this.

"Tomorrow then, Kid."

Up where he stood at the bar hardcase Dwight Chandler let out a yowl of delight and began stomping one boot to the tune the mulatto was strumming on a banjo. Chandler brought the hunk of ham he held to his mouth and ripped away with his teeth. The juice from the ham trickled down the corners of his mouth and onto his shirtsleeve. Others were enjoying the ham and sausage and some cheese supplied by the bartender.

Chiefly their pleasure was for the women being forced to drink with them, the storekeeper's wife and daughter. A few minutes ago Hazel Enright had stated her intentions to call it a night, only to be told to stay where she was. From here she knew it was only a matter of time before the outlaws got it in their heads to troop upstairs. Came this worried musing from Hazel Enright: well, you wanted a little excitement in your life and now you're gonna have to pay for it.

Most of the outlaws had pulled their chairs around to take in what was happening at the other table. Here Steve Beaudine, not all that old and pimply-faced, but all the same a killer, couldn't keep his moonstruck eyes off the lissome body under the quail-colored dress worn by the storekeeper's daughter. The hardcases drew amusement from this and the fact the older woman was getting a little tipsy. His arm snugged around Connie Watson's shoulders, Petrie kept his other hand busy refilling her glass or laying his rough fingers across her bare arm. Despite his talk of how pretty she was, really her oval face was plain as an old plow shear, though the whiskey she'd been forced to drink had brought back some color to her face.

Under different circumstances, Petrie got to thinking, she would be crawling all over him. There was a sensuousness about her that her husband couldn't satisfy. But there was her daughter squatting on the next chair. He said with a lusty tremor in his voice, "Bet when you was younger you had your pick of men in this valley."

"There . . . there was one or two . . ."

Now a shape appeared where the door had been. Chandler up at the bar was the first to take in the storekeeper striding in gripping a shotgun. "Get over there with the others," he barked at Chandler. Rainwater had plastered Aaron Watson's hair down and it shone on his thick black beard and on the weapon he was carrying. "You scum . . . you think you can come in here and just take over! Connie, you and Karen, get over here."

"Hold on," the Kid said even as under the table his hand was curling around a gun butt.

"No! No talk from you scum! That's right, Connie, ease away from the table now . . ."

Back where he'd been plunking tunes on the banjo, Inky Braxton realized the man wielding the shotgun hadn't seen him. Slipping to his feet and not bothering to discard the banjo, the mulatto came up along the studded side wall. As the storekeeper's wife blundered to her feet, she was a screen between Braxton and her husband. The mulatto pulled out his six-gun, unmindful of the fact that he'd risk hitting the woman, as his target was just part of the upper right chest and the storekeeper's head. The one shot hammering out of his gun sounded hellishly loud in the low-ceilinged barroom. The bullet struck the storekeeper's throat and it spun him sideways. His shotgun went off as the Kid and a couple of others opened up on the dying man, and with that Watson's wife dropped in a faint into sawdust.

The throatier roar of the shotgun still assailing their ears, the outlaws realized it was over, and some broke out laughing. Over at his table, Kid LaDuke let his gunhand flop onto the tabletop as he said slurringly, "The nerve of that meat cutter. Inky, thanks for savin' our bacon. And you, Lily gal, it's time to hit the sack."

"Not a bad idea," agreed Petrie, as he grimaced down at the storekeeper's wife. "Well, I've got me a woman." Then he was kneeling to bring her into his arms, and he went after the Kid forcing Lily Hudson up the creaking staircase.

Even as Hazel Enright was rising from the table in an attempt to vacate the saloon, a hard hand clamped onto her arm, and she blurted out, "Look, a drink is a drink . . . but I draw the line . . ."

The hardcase thumbed back the hammer on his leathered handgun and tightened his grip on her arm. "What the hell, you're a widow woman, with nobody to go home to. I figure you owe me for all them drinks, so come on, honey."

Behind his bar, the bartender knew that to interfere could see him stretched out alongside Aaron Watson. He saw the appeal for help on Karen Watson's face, but that wasn't enough for him to go for the sawn-off Greener within reach of his hand. Anguish twisted up his face, for he'd been one of those petitioning for the village to hire some kind of lawman. Once the steps quit groaning under the weight of the hardcases passing up them, lights were doused below, with the bartender cleaning out the cash drawer and locking up, to leave those women at the mercy of the outlaws as he hurried away.

Scarcely had Kid LaDuke forced Bonner's daughter into his room than he was groping to sit down on the bed, so drunk everything in the room seemed to be spinning around. He braced back with both hands palmdown on the narrow bed and grinned over at Lily Hudson. "You and me . . . is gonna have some fun . . ."

"How's this for fun!" came her taut response. She slammed the water pitcher down at his grinning face, and LaDuke fell over without making a sound.

Quickly Lily went to get his six-guns, and she held them on quivering legs, her ears keening to what was going on in the other rooms. Someone threading down the hallway brought her up to the door, and then a door slammed. The glare of lightning came through the only window to show LaDuke still stretched out on the bed and Lily going to the window. It opened hard; she tossed out one of the Kid's guns, and it thudded down beside an overturned bucket amidst the litter and weeds on the ground out back of the saloon.

Crouching out, she tucked the revolver under her coat to protect it from the slanting rainfall before letting go to drop down. Picking herself up, Lily ran around to the front of the saloon. She found that the bartender had closed the place down, which brought her breaking at a run for the livery stable. All she wanted to do was saddle up a horse and make it to the last town they'd passed.

The horses began stirring around in their stalls when she opened one of the front doors only to have the wind snatch it out of her grasp and slam it against the red-painted wall. She picked up a blanket and the saddle under it, and the racehorse tethered alone in a stall lashed out with a back leg.

"Settle down," Lily gasped as she veered away toward the next stall. The horse she began saddling was one the outlaws had stolen from her father, and it started shying away until she spoke up. "Easy, Goldie. It's just me, girl."

"An' it's just me, Inky Braxton."

"No!" Lily screamed as she tried going for the six-gun tucked in her waistband, but he was quicker and stronger; the outlaw easily got her out into the runway.

"You woke me up," he said scoldingly. "The Kid must have passed out or you'd never have gotten away from him. That right?"

"Please, just let me go."

"You're right about somebody pulling out of here," said the mulatto, "only it won't be you." He untied a lasso from a saddle and used it to tie Lily to a support post. "I let you go and the Kid'll be after me. Damn fool's all mixed up inside . . . all

109

kinds of crazy . . ."

"Then you should let me go. You know he's going to kill me . . . please . . ."

From here on Inky Braxton ignored Lily as he finished saddling the mare. His decision to break away had been building ever since they'd come up here. Instead of messing around with that racehorse, they should have hit some banks in those Flathead Valley cowtowns. But that wasn't the worst of it. Kid LaDuke was losing control of his men. Coming onto crunch time, Kid; you against Cunny.

Bundled up in his yellow rain slicker, the hardcase walked the mare up the dirt runway. Some riders had just come in, he realized. He swore at their intrusion as he swung into the saddle, but he refrained from leaving the livery stable upon noticing they were holding in front of the Lookout Saloon. Then one of them shouted,

"Kid, it's me, Wiley Sheldon. You in there?"

An upstairs window was flung open. "About time you got back."

"Where's the Kid?"

"What the hell you think? Sacked out."

"We ran into that tracker. Worse than that, there's a posse coming after us, some thirty, forty men."

"How far back?"

"I figure they'll pull in here around noon or after. You wake the Kid," went on Wiley Sheldon as he noticed the others were riding on toward a livery stable.

With the rain pounding down they failed to notice the mulatto fading into the darkness behind some buildings. To attempt going over Lookout

110

Pass, Braxton realized, would be too much of a risk. He'd head back through this valley, and from here head south, to a place where a man didn't have to suck this thin mountain air into his lungs.

"Kid, I figure you're the joker in this deck. Everybody wants a piece of your mangy hide."

Chapter Eleven

With the sun bursting out from behind scattering clouds, the day began to warm into a promise of reaching the seventies. Obediently Bonner Hudson's claybank followed the mountain trail, which was unmarred by other riders, although Bonner had come across the track of a deer and some drifting cattle. Down more in the valley and on this same trail lay the town of De Borgia, which he'd ridden into just after sunup. What he'd learned there hadn't been all that helpful, just of a few riders passing through in the past week. As he was just a stranger himself it was about what he expected. But he had told the local law to expect a posse to be showing up.

Gradually the valley floor was giving way to rock shelfings and narrowing upward. Off to the left, willows, aspens, and alders formed a screen along a creek, with a cottonwood rising over this serpent of brush, but closing on the trail where Bonner rode were pine trees out of which fell an occasional raindrop. Inwardly there was a muting of his senses, out of which he listened for the sounds of the mountain, the scolding of birds, or the sound that crackled the branches against the rustle of the wind. In this, the beginnings of the mountain forest, were ripples caused by critters living here, so any alien intrusion or disturbance would carry down to Bonner. As he knew anyone passing through this high wilderness would churn up as much noise as he churned up landscape.

"Just be quiet and listen," murmured Bonner as he stared up at where the creek came gorging out of a narrow break in the mountain too small to be called a canyon.

The creek water that came foaming out had formed an alluvial fan, an outspread sloping deposit of boulders, gravel, and sand. A mist rose to veil a few trees clinging tenaciously to rock crevices or on fringes of bank. Rushing waters made a throaty sound which brought Bonner to the sudden realization there was a difference in the sounds coming from uptrail. He reined off the trail to bring the claybank under a Douglas fir, but Bonner didn't bother to reach for his sidearm.

After a wait of about a half hour, the tracker's patience was rewarded by the appearance of a horseman. Right away Bonner recognized the mare. The man astride her was slouched, with a sleepy expression on his ebony face, so it was a shock to Inky Braxton when ghosting out onto the trail came Bonner Hudson.

"Wha . . . the . . ."

"Didn't mean to spook you," Bonner said quietly, and trying to keep the anger from showing. He had

113

every right to take out the Negro, but doing so wouldn't help him find his daughter. "How far is it to Salt Creek?"

"About" — Braxton twisted in saddle and pointed at some distant point on the mountain — "five miles beyond where you see that ugly gash on that cliff. Trail gets worse further west you go."

"Nice hoss you're riding, mister."

"Got an easy gait; just bought it too. Back there at Salt Creek."

"That so. Along with that bill of sale it might help you to know that mare is called Goldie."

The mulatto made a move for his gun, had it clearing leather when Bonner's Colt Frontier bucked in his hand. As the slug ripped into Braxton's chest, Braxton realized he should have gone the other way out Lookout Pass. He folded out of the saddle and dropped into the drying mud of the trail. Most of his weight had come down on his right shoulder. He knew it was broken, and he began cursing weakly in the shock of what had just happened. He managed to roll onto his back, his mud-splattered six-gun lying within reach. It struck him that blood was seeping through the front of his shirt. A weak laugh showed a mouthful of bony white teeth. Conscious of the man who'd just shot him swinging down to move over and kick the gun away, Braxton muttered weakly, "The Kid's scared to death of you . . . Mr. Tracker. Your . . ." As pain lanced away from the chest wound, it came to the mulatto that he was dying, and the fear of this flared briefly in his eyes. "Your daughter . . . she's still alive . . ."

"Where are they?"

"Back there, holed up . . . Salt Creek . . ."

"I expect they'll be pulling out of there. But where?"

Bonner's words were answered by the mulatto's death rattle. "Damn," Bonner said as he straightened up to holster his sidearm. "You should have winged him." But Bonner Hudson's bitter anger had caused him to go for the killing wound.

It took some time for him to whistle the mare in, and even then he had to use his lasso. From here he managed to load the mulatto on the mare, thinking that by rights he should leave the body out here. Snugging the rope around the inert body of the outlaw, he brought the mare over to tie its reins to a tree branch. Going to where he'd ground-hitched the claybank, he opened a saddlebag and lifted out a bottle of whiskey. This was an occasion when a drink was necessary; not because he'd killed a man, but because Lily was still alive.

It must be that the mulatto had called it quits riding with Kid LaDuke, probably after those others Bonner had encountered had made it back to tell of sighting the posse.

"Four dead now," said Bonner as he recorked the bottle and put it in his saddlebag. "Less men to split that money with. This should set well with Teddy LaDuke; he was always a stingy little shit."

About a decade ago gold had been discovered in the two streams converging on the southern edges of Salt Creek. In one summer of digging the gold had been cleaned out, and the only reason for the town's existence now was that it squatted right on the lower reaches of a canyon spilling up to Lookout Pass. Weeds and buffalo grass grew high around deserted buildings.

The view Bonner had of Salt Creek was away from the trail and on a shelf of high ground where a few trees had taken hold. He didn't need his field glass to know that the rotting freight wagons on the flats below him marked the outskirts of town. He counted smoke pouring from the chimneys of five houses, but it troubled him that he hadn't seen anybody. An eerie quietness about the buildings kept Bonner from going on in. That building with a haystack behind it had to be a livery stable. A place this small didn't have the comforts of a church, but northerly just this side of a bluff crosses marked a cemetery. Oftentimes places like this could hang on for years in the hopes another gold mine would be discovered.

No sense putting it off any longer. He worked his way down through the trees, as he'd decided to go in on foot. If the outlaws were still here, any rider coming in from the east would do so under their guns.

Down by the wagons, he set a course further in to a shed and the buggy by it. When he rounded a shed corner he saw some chickens scratching away in the barren yard of a house with curtains adorning its windows. The house was just north of the main drag, not set on a street, but, like the other

116

buildings in Salt Creek, placed there at the builder's whim. The worn track leading away from the house took him to the main road and the protection of an elm tree. He passed under the tree to throw a shadow toward the mercantile store owned by the late Aaron Watson. Then it came to Bonner that what he was hearing was a chorus of voices.

"Sound awful sad," was his wondering comment.

First some horses pulling a wagon emerged from around the Lookout Saloon. Next came a line of people on foot, and he realized it was a funeral procession, and something else. Bonner checked the impulse to turn as he heard the all-too familiar sound of a Winchester being levered.

"You've got a helluva nerve coming back here! Turn you sonofabitch so you can face the man that's gonna send you to Hades." His face a damning visage of pent-up hatred, bartender Elroy Hattan stood in the protection offered him by the recessed entryway of the mercantile store. The way they'd killed Aaron and violated his womenfolk, just scummy thieves too as they'd about cleaned the saloon out of corn whiskey.

"Hold your fire, Elroy."

"Hazel, you keep out of this." Now with the outlaw facing him, Elroy Hattan realized he'd never seen the man before. But wait, hadn't some more ridden in last night. "Mister, you just use your left hand to unbuckle that gunbelt. An' dammit, elevate your right hand, away up there."

"Sure," Bonner Hudson said with a measured calmness. "You, ma'am, and you others, I figure

117

Kid LaDuke pulled in here. Reason I know is he's kidnapped my daughter. Don't have it pinned to my shirt, but there's a badge in my fob pocket testifying to me being a deputy sheriff."

"Just where the hell is your hoss, mister?"

He gazed at Elroy Hattan. "Reason I didn't ride in is I figured they'd still be here. Left my hoss back yonder; and another hoss packing a dead body, that of a Negro I ran into back a piece."

"That," said Hazel Enright as she came closer, "must be the mulatto. They raised hell about his taking off after he'd tied the woman they brought along in the livery stable. Lily, she's your daughter?"

"How is she?"

"Hasn't been treated all that kindly."

"Dammit, Hazel, he's got to be one of them."

"No, there's something about him."

"You'll find my claybank is wearing the same brand as the mare the mulatto was riding; her name's Goldie. Just want to say, folks, that a posse isn't all that far behind."

"Hazel, you take his guns. Do it!" Elroy Hattan was still too mindful of all that had happened, so full of anger that he couldn't let go of his notion of Bonner being an outlaw. "Otis, go bring those hosses in. Them brands don't match up . . ."

Around a tired smile Bonner fingered out the badge given him by Sheriff Harvey Black, which he handed to the woman backing off and holding his gunbelt. "When did they pull out?"

"Early this morning. Heading into the canyon."

118

This part of the valley was a higher mass of land throttling up to become part of the surrounding mountains. If the Kid knew anything about horses, he must realize the racehorse couldn't take this hard pounding. He raised his eyes to the patches of snow way up past timberline. Beyond to a mellow blue sky. It seemed peaceful, yet Bonner knew it would be up there someplace that Kid LaDuke would stop. The upper reaches of the pass could be held by one man with a rifle.

The passage of Otis Kincaid back into town astride Bonner Hudson's claybank brought the bartender out into the street. He made no comment when Bonner lowered his hands, as they took in the second horse, and most of the men came away from the wagon bearing the dead storekeeper's body. Kincaid walked both horses up to Bonner and said loudly, so that the women hanging behind the wagon could hear, "Same brand on both horses." He got down heavily, after which he led the horses over and tied the reins of the claybank to a hitching rack in front of the mercantile store where Elroy Hattan was still keeping a watchful eye on Bonner.

His face registering the decision he'd just made, the bartender said grumpily, "You brought the mulatto in; you bury him."

Bonner Hudson tended to burying the mulatto after the body of Aaron Watson had been laid to rest in the cemetery. Once in a while he glimpsed someone looking up the barren slope at him, but

119

nobody came up to offer a hand at digging, which he didn't expect anyway. Nor did he bother saying a prayer over the mulatto's grave in departing.

When he got down to leave the shovel at the livery stable, to his surprise the woman he knew only as Hazel was waiting for him. He dismounted by the watering trough, where he left the shovel, then leaned to the task of washing the sweat and loamy dirt from his face and bare forearms.

"Thought you'd be hungry."

As he opened a saddlebag to pull out a spare shirt to use to dry himself, his flaring smile was for the basket she carried. "You're most kind."

"Last night," she began hesitantly, "well, they wouldn't let us leave the saloon. That LaDuke, he was the worst one, treating your daughter like so much dirt." Hazel Enright went on from there to tell the rest of it, how after they'd been taken upstairs, more outlaws had come riding in. That it was here Kid LaDuke came storming out of his room to say that Lily Hudson was gone. "They found her tied up in the stable, Mr. Hudson. The mulatto must have done that."

"Lily, how did she look?"

"She's tough as they come. I wish I were a man . . . I'd go with you."

"Passed through here five, six years ago. Up into that pass is quite a climb. I figure that's where they'll be. The deal, Hazel, is Kid LaDuke figures to get paid for giving back that racehorse. I hope Lily's included in that swap."

"What do I tell that posse when it pulls in?"

120

"That up there might be the end of the line." Once he was in the saddle, she passed Bonner the basket, which he hooked over his saddle horn. "What keeps you in a place like this?"

"Until all of this happened I didn't have the courage to clear out of here. Reckon I just gave up. Wish . . . wish there was more I could have done for your daughter . . ."

"That you care is what counts."

The canyon was like most except that it cut up more sharply into the lower rocks of the mountain. The outlaws, by the tracks Bonner found, had been the first ones to travel upon the narrow lane since it had rained. He took the wending climb at a walk and helped himself to the food in the basket, a few sandwiches and some dried fruit. Further along he pulled the claybank toward a creek and refilled his canteen.

On the move again, he had this strong feeling that he was being watched, which only confirmed his suspicions as to Teddy LaDuke's next gambit in this game of rustling and sudden death.

The afternoon wore on under a sudden onslaught of summery wind. The wind would cause a lot of changes in the way the birds of the mountains acted, and Bonner listened to it now moaning through the pines. When he came to a level place, he reined over and stepped from a low boulder to the cone-strewn ground. More anxious than thirsty, he reached back for his field glass. He scoped in on the track that eased around boulders and sometimes disappeared around a mountain wall, and then he saw to his astonishment the man he sought taking his ease in the shade of a fallen log, just Kid LaDuke by his lonesome. Through the field glass he tried to find the rest of the gang or get a glimpse of Lily. It was when he sighted in on LaDuke again that he spotted the white piece of cloth dangling from a tree limb.

Sighted me long before this, Bonner pondered. *Why the Kid is there, he wants to tell me just how this is going to be played out. Still, he's a nervy little shit.* Bonner knew too that he could go on at a faster gait, as the outlaws would hold their fire.

The claybank responded eagerly when it was brought into a lope, but the man astride it was torn by all that had happened since Kid LaDuke had decided to come back. One killing after another seemed to be the Kid's trademark, from Salt Creek clear back into the Flathead Valley. Bonner could tell he was closing in from the way birds were flitting away from trees just uptrail.

Suddenly Kid LaDuke was coming out onto the track to wait for the tracker, who ducked under some low branches, with an inborn wariness taking in not only the Kid but everything in sight. He knew the Kid would be positioned so that he could be seen by those holding Lily. Thoughts of his daughter brought anger flickering into Bonner's eyes, but when he was close enough to swing down he pulled a taut mask across his face. "Long time, Kid."

"You're getting some gray hairs." LaDuke smiled. "See you're still forking the same hoss, though."

"Like me it's seen better years. I've heard bad reports about how you've been treating my daughter."

"She's alive is all you've got to know. Gets to you, don't it, that I've got the edge."

"How do you want this handled?"

"Simple, Bonner. Dancy's money will get his hoss back."

"Lily?"

"She'll be the one riding that hoss right through here. But the deal is Dancy's got to bring that money up yonder. See that tree burned by lightning? One of my men'll be down there by it, the rest up there with Lily and me. Soon's I'm handed the money, I'll make the switch."

"That's like having you shuffle the cards when everyone else is out of the room."

"That's the way it's gonna be, Bonner. You go tell Dancy Stuart that, that he'd better have the money. Or his damned hoss Daredevil gets killed."

Bonner Hudson threw the Kid a cold nod. "You hurt my daughter, Teddy, and I'll hunt you clear down to Cape Horn, and beyond if necessary. One other thing, I insisted that Dancy bring that money along."

"Wanted to pull a fast shuffle, uh?"

"Not so much because of his racehorse, but I figure Lily's worth a heap more than that. I expect that posse'll be there when I get back to Salt Creek."

"Hope that it is. Be expecting you back tomorrow." Kid LaDuke allowed a big grin to show. "Lily sends her love."

If he expected to provoke anger out of Bonner Hudson it didn't work. After mounting up, Bonner simply reined his horse around and let it canter downtrail.

"That money better be here tomorrow," the Kid called after him. "Dammit, Bonner, you never did listen to me." He spun around and stalked toward his horse, and even though he held Bonner's daughter captive, he felt that somehow Bonner Hudson held the upper hand. "Damn him, that arrogant sonofabitch."

Chapter Twelve

The posse had thinned out considerably by the time it reached Salt Creek. All because Dancy Stuart didn't seem to understand you could push men just so far. Even during the rainstorm, when sheet lightning was lancing around them, the rancher insisted they keep riding. By the time they reached the St. Regis River crossing two of Dancy's cowhands had quit, with the sheriff faring worse than that, down to seven men.

Then tragedy had struck when they were swimming their horses across the creek. Downstream had swept a fallen cottonwood, sighted by Sheriff Harvey Black as the tree came bobbing around a riverbend, but not by Carl Hanna, who clung tightly to the mane of his horse. The sheriff had shouted a warning drowned out by the roaring river waters, then the massive roots of the cottonwood were hovering over Hanna, who was just now aware of the danger. Harv Black could still hear Hanna's frenzied scream, and just like that both horse and man were gone, with others narrowly avoiding the juggernaut of tree sweeping by them. They didn't bother drying off but continued on to De Borgia, where it was learned Bonner Hudson had passed through. But it was in De Borgia that Sheriff Black took charge, holding everyone there so's they could dry their clothing and see to their saddle rigging and horses.

Coming out of the Lookout Saloon to watch them ride in was Elroy Hattan. What he saw was a tired bunch of riders. He could pick out cowhand from townsman, drawn faces marked by stubble that told of not shaving for at least a week. But at least the law was here in the form of that big fellow and three others wearing badges. Hattan took in Hazel Enright watching the arrivals from the front porch of her clapboard house, and out of the livery stable came Kincaid, the tines of the fork he carried sparking from late afternoon sunlight. Drifting in were others, and some children. The bartender had been appointed as spokesman for the town, a chore he didn't relish.

Hattan looked about for Connie Watson or her daughter, and got to remembering that ever since the funeral both women had kept to their house. Along with mourning the death of the only man in their family, they were faced with the fact everyone in Salt Creek knew what those outlaws had done to them. In Elroy Hattan's interpretation of the law hereabouts, every damned one of those outlaws should be castrated before being taken out to do some skydancing. They'd made Salt Creek a sorrier

126

place than it was before. They'll leave, Connie and her daughter. Maybe some others.

Coming in to stand by the bartender was Otis Kincaid still clutching the pitchfork. "Wonder how some of those horses made it this far." He was counting heads, as he knew they'd avail themselves of his livery stable. He wasn't one to complain, even though those outlaws had left without dropping off one thin dime. "Money on the hoof for both of us."

"Lawmen don't pay," agreed Hattan, "no sense even attending church." And now he had a howdy for the sheriff and Dancy Stuart pulling away from the rest of the posse and reining up by the hitching rack.

The sheriff said as he hunched forward to dismount, "You're still here."

"Yup," said Elroy Hattan, "as I recall you came through summer before last. Your tracker passed through this morning."

Around a nod Sheriff Black said, "I couldn't help noticing the fresh-turned dirt up at your cemetery . . ."

"Must have been those damned outlaws," said Dancy Stuart as he swung down. Tying up, he inquired, "That livery stable still open?"

"Never closes."

The rancher took in the pitchfork and the manure clinging to Kincaid's shoes. "Hostler, I want my horse watered and curried down; some sweet feed if you've got it."

"Out here the amenities of high livin' aren't ob-

127

served all that much," snorted Otis Kincaid. "There's my livery stable." He held there as Sheriff Black introduced the man with him as Dancy Stuart, of how the rancher's racehorse had been stolen. Kincaid knew that here was another big rancher. He'd been a rancher himself, on a small spread up north of De Borgia. Running the livery stable gave him something to do besides sitting around whittling away at a hunk of wood and feeling sorry for himself. He had a little money tucked away, and he had his self-respect, so he didn't need someone like Dancy Stuart to come in here and turn his crank, so to speak. His ire raised, Otis Kincaid hawked out tobacco juice to have it splatter over the front hoof of the rancher's horse, and with that he ambled back to his place of business.

Harv Black fought back the grin as he set in behind the hostler, the bronc nuzzling at his shoulder. When he got to the water trough by the stable, he removed the bridle while taking in Stuart waving his son over to take his horse. The rest of them rode over, and there was little talk as they tended to horses, who were tired from the long haul out of the Flathead Valley. Just standing there, the pass looked higher to Harvey Black, and about it was a darkness that became ominous as daylight faded away. "Bonner, I hope you're still hanging in there."

"Harv, you worry too much," came Jim Bob Benham's quiet voice. "Have you talked it over with Dancy as to how the exchange is to be made . . ."

"It's Dancy's hoss and Dancy's money. But . . . until we hear from LaDuke . . ."

* * *

"You know your jurisdiction doesn't extend over here."

"Jurisdiction is something Kid LaDuke uses to his advantage," the sheriff replied.

Just the pair of them were at the bar, Sheriff Harvey Black standing at the back end and behind it, swiping with a towel at a glass, was bartender Elroy Hattan. Hattan had lighted extra lamps as the rest of the posse had scattered to the tables. He couldn't help staring down at the floor out in front of the bar where Aaron Watson had been killed. Fresh sawdust covered some bloodstains he'd been unable to scrub away. Lacking a coroner as well as a town marshal, all they could do was to put the storekeeper's body in a pine box and see to a proper burial. If it was him, pondered Elroy Hattan, would he have had the courage to do the same? "The way Aaron Watson died," he murmured. "It was plumb suicide him coming in here. Afterwards was the shameful part."

"Don't go blaming yourself for what happened."

"Reckon I could at least have gotten some men together and come back. But, dammit, I just locked up and slunk on home."

"Like you told me, Mr. Hattan, most of the able-bodied men were away working at ranches. Had you tried with some others, Kid LaDuke would have relished adding a few more notches to his guns. Those hardcases were just like a plague of locusts passing through."

129

"Yup, I suppose so. You surprise me, a sheriff spouting all this Biblical talk—"

Harv Black's eyelids flickered down as his jawline hardened, for in him was a hatred for Teddy La-Duke that went back a long way. When he picked up the shot glass, it was to down its contents with a quick flicking of his wrist, and he set the shot glass down hard and said, "Fill 'er up. 'Forgive thine enemies,' the Good Book says. Damned if I'll ever forgive LaDuke." He stared away for a moment, trying to pick out Dancy Stuart as he wanted to talk to him, then he remembered Dancy going up to his room.

His reminiscing on this spilled out at the bartender. "Probably's up there counting all that money."

"Forty thousand just to get that hoss back?" He set a bottle down to have the sheriff reach for it. "A man can work all his life and never make near that much."

Harv Black grimaced. "Maybe we should start robbing banks, Mr. Hattan. As all we are are servants to folks not caring all that much."

The coal oil lamps in the Lookout Saloon beamed yellow light upon log walls touched with a coat of varnish. The main bar was one large room with a few windows chinked with clay. A few old cowboy hats were tacked up to the rafters, one with a note pinned to its brim claiming that it had been worn by the notorious outlaw Harry Longabaugh. The food on a back table had been paid for by money put up by both Harv Black and rancher Stuart and partaken of by both those who'd ridden in and locals dropping in to tell their version of what those outlaws had done. Some were playing pinochle or stud poker, a way to get their minds off what tomorrow would bring.

Sheriff Black's trio of deputies were settled in around a table by the front door, with them two cowhands from the Double S, and Otis Kincaid and another local. They'd been discussing the tragedies of the killing here at Salt Creek, the string of dead bodies Kid LaDuke had left behind.

Walt Grisham had the floor as he drawled, "Long's I've been a lawman I've never seen anything to match this. Alone I don't believe Teddy LaDuke would have had the guts to steal that Daredevil, much less even hold up an ice cream parlor."

From Jim Bob Benham: "Don't underestimate the Kid." His eyes crinkled by lines gouging into his cheekbones went to everyone at the table. "As a lot have. Remember, Walt, that bull Stan Bradley had up at his ranch, meanest thing I ever seen on four hoofs." He paused to sip at his stein of beer.

The deputy sheriff followed the slant of Rick McPherson's stare over to a back table where the rancher's son, Kelsay, was playing poker. Jim Bob knew the bone of contention between these young men was Lily Hudson, though on the long ride over here they'd never spoken to one another. The way Kelsay Stuart was throwing out smiles and buying drinks around as he played could be excused for youthful ignorance, but Jim Bob could tell it was getting to Danny.

131

"Well, what about this bull, Jim Bob?"

"As I said that bull had a mean streak. Stomped and gored two other bulls before Stan Bradley brought it in and kept it penned in one of his barns. Kept everyone awake at night with its bellowing. Until a couple of waddies decided to get rid of it by mixing loco weed with some hay. You know what happened then, Walt. About that bull being sold as Stan didn't want it around anymore. They'd just got this wagon positioned out at this loading chute and some hands hazing it up the chute. When all of a sudden that bull went stark ravin' crazy. It came out of that chute to stampede over Stan Bradley holding by the wagon, just tore Stan apart before anyone could think to shoot that damned bull." With a sorrowful shake of his head Jim Bob looked about.

"Kid LaDuke's just as crazy," he went on. "Only he don't need any loco weed to set him off to killing."

Rick McPherson had heard the story before, and inwardly he agreed with Jim Bob. The last few days had made him realize just what Jim Bob and Grisham meant to him as maybe more than friends. And the badges they wore made them fair game for lawbreakers. When Harv Black retired, it was more'n likely Jim Bob would be the new sheriff, and Rick knew being a deputy for Jim Bob would be to his liking. Again he took in the situation at Kelsay Stuart's table, knowing that he should have spoken to Kelsay out on the trail. But he hadn't, as he knew Kelsay would take it wrong. Think I'm trying to muscle in between him and Lily, he thought.

Rick felt a hand touch his shoulder, before the sheriff said to him and his other deputies, "I'm turning in. We'll pull out early again. But before we do I'm going to iron out things with Dancy."

Coming to their table was the raucous laughter of Kelsay Stuart, who was bragging loudly that he'd just won another pot. "Another round here, dammit."

His shout to the bartender broke the rhythm of what was going on at the other tables, with Kelsay Stuart drawing a lot of resentful glances, but he had drunk just enough to be on the ragged edge of recklessness. Kelsay's uncaring laughter rang out again. This time Rick McPherson kicked up from his chair to cut an angry wedge through the sawdust and around another card table.

The smile in Kelsay's eyes faded away when he saw McPherson coming, but he held to the chair. He had little regard for McPherson, the son of a sharecropper, even though they'd gone to school together. Rick McPherson, so shy you couldn't get a word out of him even though he was standing there with a mouthful of horse manure; he chuckled to himself thinking about it. Then Rick setting his cap for Lily. But somehow this was a different Rick McPherson looming over his table, the face of the deputy etched in angry lines, and Kelsay blustered,

"You got a problem, McPherson?"

"You don't care, do you . . ."

"What the hell you talkin' about, McPherson?"

With his anger boiling over, Rick simply reached

133

across the table to hook both hands in the front of Kelsay's shirt. He yanked the son of Dancy Stuart across the tabletop, scattering cards and poker chips and drinks. The other poker players pulled their chairs out of the way. He didn't let Kelsay rise, but held him there, and then Rick rained a couple of backhanded blows across Kelsay's face, Rick's voice ringing out, "About Lily . . . you don't give a damn about her! She could be dead by now . . . and you just don't give a damn. . . ."

When Rick pulled back, it was with the realization you couldn't hear a sound in the saloon except for Kelsay Stuart moaning that he was bleeding. The first to break the silence was Jim Bob Benham's gravelly voice and the scraping of his chair as he said, "Getting on to eleven o'clock, at least bedtime for me."

The sheriff picked up on it. "Yup, I expect we'll be leaving damned early." He came over to Rick McPherson, but his concern was for Kelsay Stuart sliding back into his chair. Everyone in the valley knew about Kelsay's hot temper, but whatever he was about to say didn't come out, because a voice Harvey Black had last heard back in Big Fork brought him and everyone there swinging to look at the batwings.

Bonner Hudson had just pulled in, in time to tie up, and then watch the brief altercation from just outside the batwings. "I'm glad somebody is concerned about my daughter. Harv, we've got to talk."

"Sounds like you ran into the Kid—"

"Yeah, we had an encounter. Where's Dancy?"

134

"Upstairs in his room. Walt, go tell Dancy that Bonner is back."

Bonner Hudson shucked out of his coat as he followed after the sheriff heading for an unoccupied table. Bonner's nod took in everyone there. He was tired, that showed in the way he walked. A quiet aside from the sheriff brought Rick McPherson out of the saloon to see to stabling Bonner's horse. Settling in around the table were the sheriff, Bonner, and Jim Bob Benham.

Sheriff Black asked worriedly, "Did you see Lily?"

"Nope, but she's still alive. Tomorrow, that's when we're to make the exchange. Way up in Lookout Pass."

"Shouldn't be any problem."

"When you're dealing with Teddy LaDuke anything can happen."

Chapter Thirteen

When they'd pulled out of Salt Creek at first light, clouds were obscuring the upper reaches of Lookout Pass. Just looking at those gray, vague clouds made a man think of winter. But by mid-morning they were breaking away to reveal more and more of the upper reaches of the canyon.

Bonner Hudson wished the clouds would have held in, but they hadn't, and it seemed to him even the weather was playing into Teddy LaDuke's hands. Another worry was that Dancy Stuart felt it hadn't been necessary for everyone to come along.

Out front were Sheriff Harvey Black and his deputies, riding two abreast. Then it was Bonner, back of him Dancy and his son Kelsay. Strung out further back came three cowhands Dancy had asked along. They were mingled in with two from Big Rock, and to everyone's surprise Elroy Hattan had asked to come along.

Before leaving, Bonner had discussed this with Harv Black, and then he'd simply let the sheriff tell Hattan he was welcome to come. As Bonner saw it, Elroy Hattan figured he had something to prove. But when they got in closer, he meant to make sure the bartender stayed back a little.

Bonner Hudson doubted that this would be handled smoothly. Would the Kid just let Lily go? Once that happened, the Kid had to know he planned to keep after him until one of them was dead.

The sun warming his back took away some of Bonner's tiredness. The wind was higher up in the canyon, chasing amongst the tangled gray webbing of clouds, breaking them apart. He heard the nearby chirping of birds without thinking too much on it, for he had set his honed senses to places higher up in the pass. By his reckonings they were still a couple of hours away from where he'd encountered Teddy LaDuke.

The sheriff held up, then walked his bronc alongside Bonner's. "You taught the Kid how to track. Meaning, Bonner, that you've been inside his head . . ."

"Tracking's one thing, Harv. Funny, but when I saw him up there, he looked about the same. Still got that baby face; only babies don't kill."

"None I know of. Maybe he figures this'll be like before. That we won't keep after him. Should have, but I figured the law down in Utah would take him out." Sheriff Black took out a cigar and rolled it around in his mouth. Then from the same pocket he found a match, struck it into flame against his saddle horn, and lit the cigar, this while eyeing the man at his side. "I've got to say it, Bonner. I just don't think he plans to let your daughter go."

"Gave me his word he would. Got to cling to that for now."

* * *

When they came around a bend, the pass opened up to show the high rocks guarding it, and just how narrow it was. The track came up at more of an angle, and it was hard and bouldery. It seemed as if it had never rained up here. The line of horses was more stretched out, as Bonner judged by the sun it was around noon. Coming to Bonner were snatches of conversation and the rushing of the creek, toward which he saw Dancy Stuart reining his horse, with the pines by the creek cutting off the glare of the sun.

They set about watering their horses, and some of them brought food out of their saddlebags. But not Bonner Hudson, or Rick McPherson standing next to Bonner's claybank. Together they gazed through the branches at the pass, where some of the rocks twinkled to tell of minerals embedded in them, and there were faded-out patches of snow further up the mountainside.

"You think a lot of my daughter . . ."

Embarrassed about this, Rick McPherson rubbed at his neck and shaped a half-grin. "Guess I never told Lily that. Should have, I expect."

"I see you've been avoiding Kelsay Stuart."

"Trying to, Mr. Hudson. I just hope this works out."

Now Dancy Stuart moved over, with Bonner nodding at the rancher, who said, "Shouldn't be too much further. I know they've been watching us. I figure some of us should hang back. Otherwise La-Duke might decide to take off again."

"You're handling the money."

"I've given my saddlebags to Sheriff Black. But I intend to go along to where we make the exchange."

"Then it'll be the three of us. Well, no sense idling here any longer. See that outcropping of rock up there? Beyond that bend in the road we'll come to a bigger stand of trees. The trail widens some, where I palavered with the Kid. About a hundred yards further up is that dead pine tree, and a lot of open ground running up to it. Teddy LaDuke could forget we're coming in under a flag of truce and just open up. But I'm gambling he won't. You still want to go along, Dancy?"

"Seems I've no choice in the matter."

Reining out first was Bonner Hudson, his hat brushing against some branches so that he had to settle it over his sweat-dampened hair again. He didn't look back when another horse came loping up, and he expected it to be the sheriff. But it proved out to be the bartender, Elroy Hattan, bouncing in the saddle and gripping the reins with both hands. Under the glaring sunlight Hattan had been forced to take off both his coat and vest, and sweat stained his cotton shirt. He had on a brown derby, from under which he licked anxiously at beads of sweat touching upon his upper lip.

"I guess the sheriff told you part of why I came along, Mr. Hudson."

"He did," murmured Bonner.

"You've got to understand, I ain't no top hand at riding. Nor handling a gun, for that matter. Salt Creek's got no mayor—so they elected me spokesman."

"Reckon you're here defending the honor of your town then, Mr. Hattan."

He grasped at what Bonner had just said. "You could say that. But that's not it, exactly. It . . . it was seeing your daughter back there, knowing . . . knowing that I could have done something . . . but didn't . . ."

"Elroy, you've got nothing to prove to me," Bonner said gently. Last night's altercation at the Lookout Saloon settled into his thoughts. That if only Lily could have been there to see the true character of Kelsay Stuart, that for damnsure Kelsay had no love for her. But she was sure going to be told of this, and if not by him, by another young man willing to stand up for her. "You saw Lily in the saloon?"

"A spunky woman, your daughter. Got more moxie than me, I reckon."

It was here, as they came to the bend in the road pointed out by Bonner, that Bonner edged his horse into a lope. Here the track was more or less a narrow ledge creeping around the mountain wall, the outcropping of rock overhead, opposite a drop-off of a few hundred feet to the lower reaches of the canyon. Opening up to him now was a level stretch where the track fanned out more. Water was still contained in a pothole, and the claybank veered around this and under the trees. He let the others catch up, as just short of the high rocks guarding the mouth of the pass stood the lightning-jagged pine tree, a few of its lower branches still showing green. Bonner swung down and was rummaging in a saddlebag when Elroy Hattan rode up.

Finding a white dish towel he'd stowed there, Bonner moved deeper into the trees in search of a piece of dead branch to use as a pole for the flag of truce.

Once they had gathered in near Bonner's horse and the bartender still huddled in his saddle, Sheriff Harvey Black laid out how it would be from here on. "Me and Dancy and Bonner'll head up there. As I don't want to spook them out of here. Remember now, there's Lily Hudson; so don't be slinging lead around in case they open up. I guess . . . Dancy, you got anything to add . . ."

Dancy Stuart had a tight-lipped set to his mouth, and he merely shook his head. It was hard to tell how he felt, but there was a shortening of his reins as he set his horse after the sheriff and Bonner Hudson, striking back to the trail.

With Bonner out front, the towel held upright so that a vague wind snatched at it, they rode out from under the trees. Bonner sat straight up in the saddle and sort of relaxed, but he was checking out everything higher up in the rocks guarding the mouth of the pass. Then from out behind some rocks just beyond the dead tree came a horseman. "It isn't LaDuke," Bonner said quietly.

"Did you expect it to be?" the sheriff threw back.

Pulling up by the tree was Wiley Sheldon, who threw the approaching riders a friendly wave. He was chewing on a sprig of leaf, seemingly as unconcerned as a man just there to greet some old friends.

"So you're the tracker—"

Bonner didn't say anything as Sheriff Harvey

Black and Dancy drew up alongside. Then Bonner's eyes went to a flicker of movement higher up, and he knew the outlaws were spread out on the rocks above. He'd expected this, but was hoping the rest of the posse had worked their way into position to give them some covering fire in case Kid LaDuke was planning to pull a fast one.

"You got the money you can get your hoss back."

"I hope you haven't mistreated Daredevil," snapped the rancher. "Harv here has the money. But not until I see my horse coming down that road."

The hardcase's eyes squinted greedily at the sheriff opening one of the saddlebags out of which he removed some greenbacks, and the hardcase muttered, "It's the real McCoy all right. But there'd better be forty thousand there."

"It's all there," exploded Dancy Stuart. "Dammit, now I want to see my horse." He pursed his lips as the sheriff tossed the saddlebags to Wiley Sheldon, who placed two fingers into his mouth and whistled.

As the pounding of hoofs came through the hollow between the high rocks, the hardcase jerked his horse away from the tree and toward the track. Appearing just then was Dancy Stuart's racehorse. Unsaddled and with nobody astride it, the horse galloped downtrail, and the fears of Bonner Hudson were realized. When he took out after the hardcase just entering the narrow slot further uptrail, gunfire broke out, with a slug clipping past Bonner's head, and he had no choice but to break for cover.

Up among the protecting rocks Wiley Sheldon

was laughing as he came over the crest of the pass, and he shouted to Kid LaDuke, "That went slick, Kid."

LaDuke grinned over at Lily Hudson. "Now maybe you'll look more kindly on me, as I'm heeled. Well, open them saddlebags and let's have a look-see." Deftly he caught one of the bundles of money. "Smells so sweet."

"A lot of it here," Sheldon said.

"Then let's vamoose."

They swung their horses and the one Lily was riding away from the increasing sound of the gun battle. The Kid had given the others instructions to meet up with him at Calder on the St. Joe River. But Teddy LaDuke had different ideas about where he was heading, that being northwesterly into that Kootenai River country. From there he would work his way up into Canada. It was also his hope that Lily's father would get killed back there.

"But what the hell," he muttered, "I still aim to bed you, high and mighty Lily Hudson."

Lily Hudson flung back as she struggled against the ropes binding her to the saddle. "Go to hell, you scurvy bastard!"

Kid LaDuke's face got all twisted up in rage, and he would have struck out at her, but the hammering of guns at the top of Lookout Pass kept him to the business of galloping his bronc down into the first reaches of Idaho.

Dancy Stuart's first glimpse of Daredevil brought him wheeling the bronc under him after the race-

143

horse, which was going at full gallop down the track. He'd broken away at about the same time the hardcases had opened up, his only fear being that his valuable racehorse might lose control and pile into some rocks. The sheriff shouted after the rancher to take shelter, and then it struck Harvey Black as he peeled out of the saddle to crouch in behind the dead tree that there'd been no mention at any time of Bonner's daughter.

Dancy, he just doesn't care what happens to her. Then he was busy returning the fire of the hardcases. He held a six-gun; those above were pulling the triggers of rifles. He looked about for Bonner and saw the claybank in amongst the boulders. "Never should have trusted LaDuke. Not for one second. Bonner! Can you hear me?"

A slug chipping dead bark near his head made Sheriff Black aware that to stay here was to die. He couldn't go uphill toward Bonner, and twisting his head around, he saw that his bronc had broken downtrail. There, those rocks lower down, he decided, and with that he triggered his six-gun to empty it, then spun to break away from the tree.

Pow-pow-pow—

Up on the rocky fortification two of the hardcases lowered the barrels of their rifles and smiled at the way they'd pumped bullets into the man wearing the badge. "Tore his backbone all to hell."

"Those others are working their way up here."

"No way they can get through us. Once we've hammered the hell out of them, it's off to get our share of the money. Damn, I'm gonna get wild-assed drunk an' stay that way forever."

144

Down in the pines Kelsay Stuart was the first to catch sight of the racehorse. Before he could think to mount up, some of the men working for his father got to their horses and flung themselves into their saddles. From here they unlimbered lassos and angled in to rope the racehorse, which was trembling with the fear of what was happening. "Here comes the bossman."

Just as Dancy Stuart rode in under the sheltering trees a bullet clipped a branch away, and then he was heading over to where they were holding his racehorse. He screamed out, "How is he? How's my hoss?"

"Ain't limpin' or nothin', Mr. Stuart. What do we do now, join up with the others . . ."

Indecision playing across his face as he stared through the trees at what he could see of the pass, Dancy Stuart said roughly, "No, it's Bonner's fight now. As I'm taking Daredevil home. Hold here while I go get my son."

The rancher pulled his horse around to lope it uptrail until he came upon Kelsay huddled in a low thicket of pines. Swinging down, he crouched over and said, "Come on, we're pulling out."

"What about Lily?"

"Hear me good, son. You haven't seemed all that concerned about her on the way over here. Now do you really suppose I would let my son marry someone beneath him."

"But . . . pa, I love her, I . . ."

"Like hell you do, Kelsay. Forget Lily Hudson. Now, shake a leg as we've got a long ride ahead of us."

* * *

With the afternoon winding to a close, Bonner Hudson knew it was a stalemate, and that every minute they were pinned down here meant the further away Teddy LaDuke was taking his daughter. The thought sickened him.

From his concealment in the rocks he snaked a glance downslope at Sheriff Harvey Black sprawled out in death. He assumed others had gone down, and just maybe some up above. As he lay here, he'd been counting guns, knew there were six of them, and then only five, so one must have been hit. Sometimes he could hear them shouting out to one another, but distantly. A plan had formed, bold and born of desperation. Unfolding from behind the rocks, he crouched through his rocky enclave to the claybank, which pulled away at Bonner's appearance.

"Easy, boy, easy." Here he reloaded his sidearm, leathered it to unsheathe his Winchester and make sure its chamber was full. Uncorking his canteen, he sated his thirst as all the while his eyes were probing to where he knew a rifle was being fired.

Only a damned fool would ever think up heading up in between those high rocks guarding the pass. It wasn't that long a distance, maybe a hundred yards or less, but nonetheless a gauntlet of uncertainty or even death.

"Got no choice," was Bonner's wry comment as he sought the saddle.

Behind where he sat astride the claybank and the road were more boulders and smaller pines and not

146

much else to give him concealment. But he was just about under the lip of the rocks above, and he used this cover now to walk the claybank toward the track. In his right hand he gripped both his handgun and the reins, and his left held the Winchester. The thoughts of Bonner Hudson were set on what lay ahead.

A jab of his spurs brought the claybank breaking onto the track and up it with rocky walls tight to either side. "Come on!" he urged his horse.

The first indication that he'd been spotted came when a frenzied shout was followed by leaden slugs chipping rock behind him. Another twenty yards and he would have made it, but now something slapped into the claybank's shoulder just ahead of the saddle. Somehow it keep struggling uptrack but in a faltering stride, with blood spurting out of the wound. It was darker here in this rocky slot, but not so dark that they couldn't make out the horseman. Now another gun opened up at Bonner. He knew the claybank was mortally wounded, its demise helped along by the slug it took in the flank just as Bonner vaulted out of the saddle to land somehow on his feet. He almost dropped the rifle, but held on to it as he cleared the slot and threw himself into a thicket.

"How many of them?"

"Just the one, Cunny!"

"Then take care of the sonofabitch."

One moment Bonner was busting into the thicket, the next he was slipping out of it and away into the deeper blackness under some low pines. He held in there, unmoving, letting himself get accustomed to the scraping sounds made by the hardcases as they stepped over rocky terrain in search of him. Long shadows stretched away from the trees, the sky inking into night, and the tracker made scarcely a sound as he removed his high-heeled boots and his crowned hat. He paused once to listen to boots scraping over a nearby boulder, then went back to digging with his fingers to loosen the thin, moist soil. He spread the loamy soil across his face in darkening streaks and wiped his hand across his shirtfront. He was ready. But still he held there until a curtain of deeper black touched the sky, as if someone were turning down the wick on a coal oil lamp.

Like a whispery tendril of cloud often seen at these heights, a vague movement told of something passing through a gap in the trees. The outlaw standing just where some mossy boulders formed the higher barrier of rocks guarding the pass knew he'd seen something. He could have opened up with his rifle, but didn't, as there was nothing to line his sights on. And he was standing exposed, a dark shape of low-crowned hat, just arrogant enough not to have discarded his hand-rolled, the tip of his cigarette was a beacon of vague light. From no more than ten feet away, flame belched from Bonner's six-gun. Even as the hardcase was falling, Bonner was darting in so rapidly he could have caught the tailor-made arcing toward the ground. One touch of his hand to the neck told him the outlaw was dead. And he slipped away.

Further up in the rocks only two rifles were opening up at the posse. A fact which registered with

Bonner seeking out the same men in search of him. He knew one of them was further to the south and downslope where had filtered up the whickering of horses. As he cleared a boulder, the faintest of sounds told Bonner that the other hardcase had circled back, and he bellied to the ground.

"Beaudine, is that you?"

"I'm down here. Where's Petrie?"

"Damn . . . that must have been . . ."

His Winchester bearing on the hardcase just crabbing over a boulder about a stone's throw away, Bonner centered the barrel on the man's chest. Then the rifle bucked in against his shoulder, and the hardcase folded down and went limp.

"Three to go," uttered Bonner Hudson as he levered the rifle, but held there. For he realized the firing had tapered off. They'd be coming for him now. For they feared for their horses.

There filtered up to him now the faint creaking of saddle leather from someplace in that thicket of pines lower down. He could picture that outlaw mounting up, as now Bonner heard a shod hoof strike stone. "Like a rat leaving a burning barn." He knew it wasn't Kid LaDuke, which brought anger flinting into his eyes.

He felt rather than saw the shape of a man inching downslope amongst the rocks. There came a muttered curse, as the hardcase had picked up the sound of someone riding away. Now that he'd located the one, Bonner knew the other outlaw was either further to the south or coming straight down at him. It didn't matter. He intended to kill both of them because he figured the pair of them had picked up a lot of Teddy LaDuke's bad habits, and because of what had happened to the claybank.

Came a soft whistle, a belt buckle grating onto stone, and a shape that could only be a cowman's hat. He took this in, and knew that the hardcase would make his next move to that big low-limbed pine whose green crown seemed to touch upon a twinkling star. Bonner still hadn't located the other hardcase, so he reckoned the man must be holding tight to one spot. Up came the Winchester's barrel as in by the pine moved the hardcase, close enough for Bonner to see the fear flickering out of the eyes and the whites of them flecked with red. At this distance of less than ten yards Bonner could have used his six-gun, but what he wanted was a quick, clean kill.

When his Winchester sounded, it was one rolling reverberation after another, two quick shots that threw the hardcase into the branches to hold his dead body in a swaying embrace. Just as quickly, Bonner was slipping away upward, to find the last one. It was when he got in amongst the larger rocks guarding the mouth of the pass that he purposely worked the lever on his Winchester. That jacking sound spread outward even as the last rolling sound of the shots he'd fired were fading away down the canyon.

Crouching to one knee, Bonner yelled: "There's just one of you left!"

Outlaw Dwight Chandler spun toward the sound of the tracker's voice. But he held his fire, knowing to shoot would be a mistake. This hadn't gone right at all. He should have taken off with Kid LaDuke.

150

Too late for that now. "Is that you, tracker?"

"You'll live a little longer if you tell me where the Kid's headed."

The outlaw shouted back, "West is all I know."

"You know where he went!"

His eyes stabbing above the uneven edges of the boulder, the outlaw felt a moment of panic, and as he fumbled cartridges into the chamber of his side-arm he dropped some to break out cursing. How in tarnation could one man take out Petrie and the others? This damned tracker had to be lying. Desperately he yelled, "That gal of yours, tracker, is something under the covers. Best lay I've had in a long time. You hear me, tracker!"

Dwight Chandler came up firing and still cursing his defiance at the tracker. Then he took the first of five steel-jacketed shells from the tracker's rifle, with Bonner working the lever on his Winchester in a frenzy of hate.

The acrid stench of gunpowder sweeping around him, he finally quit firing. His ears still rang from the awful hammering of his rifle. Bonner rose, to pick his way over the rocks, where he found the outlaw sprawled on his back in a jumbling of rocks.

"Damn," he finally muttered, "they die hard." Now he sank to his knees with the realization of what he'd done, that he could have made an attempt to take this one alive. Had he become like this hardcase and Teddy LaDuke, an animal lusting to kill? "Just don't know . . . just want to find my daughter—"

Chapter Fourteen

They knew it was the throaty growl of a Winchester cutting loose with a spasm of slugs, faster than any of them had ever heard a rifle fired before. Afterward came a long silence. The four of them holding under the trees, still scattered.

There came a groan of pain from Walt Grisham, and he grabbed at his arm. There was so much pain he couldn't tell if the slug was still lodged in his upper arm, where Rick McPherson had crawled over to tie his bandanna just above the bullet hole. Troubling Grisham as much as the wound was the thought of Dancy Stuart and his men pulling out, and then those two from Big Rock following suit. As for the sheriff, they weren't sure if he was still alive, because the sustained gunfire from the outlaws had kept them pinned down here under these trees. He called out to Jim Bob settled in behind a fallen tree, "What do you think?"

"Only one man I know can fire a rifle like that." Jim Bob Benham's worry was of the moon coming up to lighten up the canyon.

He wasn't sure at first, then Rick McPherson knew it was some riders coming up the track, and he slithered over to Jim Bob. "What do you make of it?"

"Dunno. But for damnsure it won't be Dancy coming back."

"Maybe it's someone from Salt Creek," Elroy Hattan threw in. He stood up despite a warning from Jim Bob and came closer. He was coatless and hanging on to a rifle. Along with the others he studied the track lowering away from them.

When two riders finally appeared, they drew up hesitantly. Then one of them shouted up his name, and Jim Bob muttered, "Cafferty was one of Dancy's hands. Guess he won't be any longer now that he's back." Now he shouted, "Frank, we're still holding here. So come on in."

Shortly both horsemen were pulling in off the track and swinging down. The other rider with Cafferty turned out to be Lem Dubay. Cafferty said, "Couldn't stomach just leaving."

"I hope that damned hoss of Dancy's breaks a leg. Anyway"—Jim Bob jerked a thumb upslope—"been quiet for about a half hour now."

"What about Bonner?"

"Just don't know about him or the sheriff. But the way I figure it, we've got to get up there. This moon . . . just got to take our chances."

"There's some cover," said Rick McPherson.

"I'm going along."

The other deputies swung to look at Walt Grisham picking himself up from the ground. They

153

knew better than to dissuade a man as stubborn as Grisham, and Jim Bob took charge quietly, by striding toward the track and easing along the north side of it. The rest spread out a little behind. They could make out the dead tree located a short distance from where the track narrowed to run up into the rocky slot.

Coming onto the tree, Elroy Hattan chanced to glance off to his right, and he exclaimed, "There's a body!" He stopped as Jim Bob broke past him, now Hattan went after the deputy. When he caught up, Jim Bob was on his knees by the body of Sheriff Harvey Black.

"Took some slugs in the back," Benham said grimly. "Damn the Kid anyway." He came erect to head back to the track, where he told of his find. "Didn't suffer much, as the way Harv was laying there a slug must have broke his backbone. So, we're almost there."

Without asking, Rick McPherson simply went on ahead. His long strides carried him up the middle of the track, which brought everyone else into a jog. Up here between the rock walls it was darker, but still enough light to let McPherson see the rounded shape of the dead horse. When he came closer he saw it was Bonner Hudson's claybank, and he took a firmer grip on his .45 Peacemaker.

"One got away and the rest are dead," a voice told them.

Rick McPherson jumped back and would have fired, but Jim Bob said loudly, "Bonner, dammit, you just gave me some more gray hairs."

Coming to stand skylined above them, Bonner Hudson said, "Where are the rest?"

"Done took off," Walt Grisham threw out. "That damned Dancy's got no sand; same goes for his son."

As everyone moved up the track, Bonner let out a bitter sigh. He should have expected this from Dancy, and in a way he had. But still it hurt, especially considering Lily wore a ring given her by Kelsay. Better finding out about him now. Coming on now, they moved onto more level ground, the flames of a campfire drawing them after Bonner heading toward it, with Bonner making the comment that he'd prowled downtrail and was pretty sure his daughter and two outlaws had left before the gun battle.

"Found their hosses down there and a lot of grub and whiskey in their saddlebags—made some coffee too."

"Just what happened up here, Bonner Hudson!" exploded Jim Bob.

"Look around you'll find five bodies. I took out four of them. Harv, he didn't have a chance. Nor did my claybank, I reckon."

"I expect none of them'll be the Kid."

Jim Bob Benham said, "So, there's coffee, but my cup's back in my saddlebag. But, Bonner, when do you plan on heading out after them?"

"I'm going along," Elroy Hattan said firmly.

Taking in the rest of them, Bonner put aside the decision he'd made to go ahead by his lonesome. What he had here were real men culled out from all who'd come along. Any bitterness he felt toward Dancy or anyone else was washed away as he looked about, at Jim Bob and McPherson, the bartender, the others.

"Angelica and I thank you . . . as does my daughter. Well, you'd best get your horses. I expect we'll start early. Only, Walt, that arm needs tending to."

"Bonner's right," said Jim Bob. "An' don't get all muley on us now."

"Expect you're right," grumbled Walt Grisham. "But when I pull out I'll pack Harv's body along back to Salt Creek."

A shooting star, and another, came blazing over the encircling rim of mountains. The sky thick with stars, and with the moon fading away. Later, after their horses were tethered nearby, there was a final settling around the campfire. A bottle of whiskey was passed around, more to ward off the encroaching chill than anything else.

"Teddy LaDuke won't be expecting us to come after him so soon. Maybe it'll be different this time."

"Lily, this has been hard on her."

Setting his eyes on McPherson, Bonner smiled as he said, "Knowing you care will mean a lot to her."

An elk with a large rack of horn broke out of the early morning mist and came to an abrupt stop in the middle of the road. It would have been a tempting target for Bonner, had he chosen to go for his

156

rifle. Under him the bronc broke stride, but he nudged a spur to its flank as the bull elk decided to vacate the road that leveled off to flow into a mountain valley.

The danger of coming down the pass at night was proven when they'd come across a horse with a broken front leg. That even an outlaw could let a horse suffer like this caused a lot of angry comments. A bullet from Bonner's gun took the bronc out of its misery. Not all that far ahead should be a man on foot. Their worry now was of the outlaw laying an ambush. If perchance they took him alive, mused Bonner, it was most likely someone would suggest using a rope. Already this had been tossed about.

The rising hulk of the mountains on their back-trail brought down a shadow that still covered them. The brush was thicker down here, and it fanned out into low pockets of broken ground. One thing in their favor was the patches of fog lifting a little. This end of the valley seemed barren of cattle or of any chimney smoke, but in most cases ranch buildings would be snugged into the mouths of canyons. It could be, Bonner voiced to Jim Bob, that if the outlaw did sight some buildings that's where he'd head.

"Know I would. Bonner, seems to be the mountain to our left tapering off into another valley."

"As I recall, you'll find a river down there, the St. Joe. There'll be a lot more breaks in the mountains ahead."

"It could be a long chase."

Bonner had the notion it wouldn't be as he

157

spurred ahead. This was a long valley and not all that wide, but there were a few settlements. To keep one jump ahead of them the Kid would have to change horses. The Kid might even hold over someplace to spend some of Dancy's money.

He set his mind back to the hoofprints left by the three horses, for just ahead the trail divided. The south fork led down between some peaks, and there in the hazy distance were cattle grazing in shortgrass. He hadn't told the others, but back about a mile he'd lost the tracks of the man on foot. Now Bonner brought his horse into a widening circle, and soon he was bringing it further to the south and east a little to scare out a steer from a thicket. That hardcase could be lurking back there where a lot of trees were spread up the lower reaches of the mountain.

"No sense wasting our time on one man," muttered Bonner as he swung the bronc around and cantered it back to the waiting horsemen. "He's back there someplace."

"I think it's more important we keep after the Kid."

Nodding, Bonner said, "That hardcase'll keep. Just like when you go fishin', you don't hook all the fish in a creek."

The road, which was just two ruts centered by grass, brought them westerly. Noon slid by, but they were more concerned with playing catch-up than chowing down, and the talk tapered off more, although the bartender let go with a complaint at times how his buttocks were painin' him. As for

Jim Bob Benham, he was getting his mind all tied up into knots over what would happen when Bonner got back home. It was him, Jim Bob knew, he couldn't just let it go what Dancy Stuart had done by pulling out. He took in the weary set to Bonner's face.

"Well," said Jim Bob as he took in the spread to the hoofprints they were following, "they ain't goin' full out. With afternoon about over, I reckon as you said, Bonner, they'll wash the trail dust out of their craws in some town. That Cataldo town, maybe."

"Cataldo, they might get that far," he said, and he added in a quieter aside to Jim Bob, "I want to take a look ahead."

The deputy sheriff took out after Bonner, loping around Elroy Hattan, who was riding alongside McPherson. He didn't catch up until they passed over an elevation. When he did, Jim Bob brought his bronc down to a jog. What Bonner said caught him by surprise.

"Cafferty? Why I've known him a long time."

"I said Frank Cafferty was an outlaw. Long time back. Don't know all that much about Dubay. But it surprised me them coming back."

"Like they said, they couldn't stomach what Dancy had done."

"Or it could be they're after the money."

Chapter Fifteen

Once Kid LaDuke got a glimpse of Cataldo he knew it was his kind of town. Sagging tiredly in the saddle, he surveyed the town from benchland north of the Coeur d'Alene River. Wiley Sheldon was just coming up through a sloping cut of rock and trees; he was not all that happy about the Kid keeping them at a gallop most of the day.

Just east of them an opening between mountain ranges revealed more peaks guarding another valley. Sheldon laid anxious eyes that way and eastward to the wide recess of valley floor. They should have changed horses back when passing through the last settlement; the one he was astride wheezed its tiredness. He'd be lucky if his bronc made it into Cataldo, and this time Wiley Sheldon would be glad to fork over some ready cash for a new horse.

Thinking of the money chased away some of his worries, and there was the tracker's daughter and what the Kid had in mind for her tonight.

Those plans had better include him, the hardcase mused. He figured they was equal partners now. So LaDuke had better think about sharing Lily Hudson's charms. He fastened bold eyes upon Lily, who was slumped on that gray, all bundled up in an old greasy hat and a coat sizes too large. Take off them accoutrements and underneath was all the woman any man could want. Alongside with some money bulging out a trouser pocket he could feel another bulge forming in his crotch, and he got to grinning.

Then it struck him about the Kid's deciding she was getting to be extra baggage. This was earlier this morning when they'd pulled up to water their horses at a creek. LaDuke's attitude was more upbeat as he'd gotten to talking about the tracker. Sheldon had to agree that Cunny and the others could keep that posse from getting through. Now as Wiley Sheldon took in the woman they held captive, there was a moment of compassion. The short piece of rope binding her wrists were tied to the saddle horn, and a rope tied to her near boot passed under the belly of the gray and looped around her other leg. It made for uncomfortable riding, but Lily Hudson had never complained, though from her radiated this aura of hatred for both him and the Kid.

Reckon the Kid'll see her dead after he's pleasured her. Seems he hates her too.

"Yessiree, Wiley, this Cataldo is big enough to have plenty of saloons."

"When d'ya figure on divvyin' up the money?"

161

"Not up here for damned sure," snapped the Kid.

Lily Hudson closed her eyes as she licked at her lower lip. Her lips were dried out and split from the sun, and she felt a little feverish. Overriding this was the dull pain emanating from the left side of her face, which was still puffed out from where LaDuke had struck her. Every muscle shouted out with a soreness she'd never felt before, but her mind was still clear, seeking a way to escape from Kid LaDuke.

"We can't take her into town, Kid."

"Yeah, I know," he muttered with a glance Lily's way. "Down there where that brush is chokin' along the river. Leave her there. Then go to that shitkickin' cowtown and a hot bath to get rid of this stink."

"And a heap of whiskey," chortled Wiley Sheldon.

The Kid, after giving their backtrail a lazy search, went ahead off the level terrace of ground spilling to either side and let his bronc pick a downward course to stir up pebbles, shaley rocks, and little puffs of dust. They looked around for a suitable campsite on the wide floodplain, which was carpeted with elm and cottonwoods fighting for survival. They soon found one closer to the river but screened from it by brush. There were some dead trees to hitch their horses to, and Lily's.

She was still in the saddle and for a moment Kid LaDuke stood looking up at her. He fondled the inside of her upper leg, his eyes all agleam with lust. "With that shiner you look like goat shit, Lily dear."

"Heard your pa was a goat," she said through lips curled up in derision, a challenge in her eyes that he didn't have the guts to end this now. *Just unlimber one of them hogirons, Kid, and take me out,* was an inner musing of Lily's. A sneer told him this. But there was LaDuke's need to have his way with her first.

"Damned bitch," he spat out as he wrapped a hand around the haft of his hunting knife. He was tempted to cut her up a little, just to see her writhe in pain, but a string of expletives served to calm LaDuke down some, as the knife cut the rope away from her near boot. Next he cut the rope tying her hands close to the saddle horn. Then he grabbed her arm and pulled her out of the saddle.

Lily landed hard at the Kid's feet, her gasp of pain springing forth from him a mocking snicker.

"You're as clumsy as yer old man; but a helluva lot prettier. Tonight is when I get a glimpse of your naked butt, Lily dear."

"What about now?"

"Simmer down, Wiley. Maybe I'll share her with you. But tonight. We'll leave our bedrolls here. While I tend to that, go rustle up some firewood. 'Cause I don't want to stumble around in the dark looking for any."

When they pulled out it was to leave their prisoner tied up. As an afterthought Wiley Sheldon

163

spread his soogans over Lily, who was sitting with her back wedged against the fallen tree, something that caused the Kid to break out laughing.

"Ya goin' sweet on her, Wiley. . . ."

Getting back on his horse, Sheldon allowed as how it got doggoned cold at night in these mountain valleys. "We might not even get back tonight, not with all that money we're packin'."

Reining his bronc through more thickets encroaching on the river, LaDuke said, "Be hard findin' this place after dark. But, yup, pard, there's the money." A jab of his spurs brought the Kid's horse bursting riverward, where as it splashed across he set smiling eyes on the town just downstream about a quarter of a mile.

The main valley road kept on south of the river, and it showed signs of recent traffic of horsemen and vehicles. From the inquiries Bonner Hudson had made at the small towns they'd passed through, he knew the Kid and another outlaw and Lily had come this way. He didn't feel that just narrowing the gap was good enough anymore. If they meant to save his daughter, they'd have to catch up. But at least he was still able to pick out, from all the other hoofprints embedded in the road, occasional signs of three, and consign them to his tracker's memory.

The day was as hot as it got this time of year, bringing recollections of the drought of '74. Despite the heat they had no choice but to push on.

164

The red ball of the sun struck in low from the west to blind them as to what lay ahead. Then when the sun did sink away, it was surprising how quickly the chill of night set in.

"What you thinking of?"

"Mostly the weather, Jim Bob. Goes from one extreme to the other."

"Cycles like that happen, Bonner. We should be about seven, eight miles away from Cataldo."

"If they go that far," Bonner pondered, "as the valley opens up to the north. Seems like the ground's chewed up ahead . . ."

" 'Pears so, and a lot of cowshit too." Jim Bob Benham held his bronc to a walk as Bonner spurred his claybank into a lope.

Frank Cafferty called out, "That'll wipe out the Kid's tracks."

When they came up to Bonner, he was holding his horse in the middle of the road surveying where at least a hundred head of cattle had passed through to the west. He lifted his eyes in the same direction and beyond to sight in on the reach of benchland northerly. Just this side he could make out the break in the chain of mountains, where the Kid could be heading. What he didn't know was of the small herd of cattle erasing the tracks left by Kid LaDuke when he veered toward the river to cross over. His decision made, Bonner swung his horse sideways so's he wouldn't have to peer into the sun.

"Cataldo, biggest town in the valley. If they keep to this road, that's where the Kid'll be."

Cataldo was deep enough in the mountains that a telegraph line hadn't reached out to it, though a petition to have one had been gotten up by the town council. The pair of riders coming in from the east had commented on this, with Wiley Sheldon the last to speak.

"Then it woulda been me shimmyin' up a pole to cut the wire. See that bank."

"The Stockgrowers Bank of Cataldo; got a fancy false front. We'll mark it for future reference."

They rode at a jog past a man coming out of the bank to lock up. Their shabby presence drew a wondering glance from the banker and a few people hurrying into stores to buy last-minute purchases—it was a little past six o'clock. Setting time for the sun wouldn't be for another couple of hours, though, and it pleased the Kid they'd reached here before dark.

He took note of the Spaniard Hotel just kitty-corner from a café and the Emerald Bar. Spreading beyond were other business places. The street was wide enough to permit the passage of at least three wagons. Their horses did not stir up any dust, and the ringing of their shod hoofs caught the eye of a woman just coming out of the hotel. One glance at their shabby, trail-dusted clothing told her they were just a couple more down-at-the-heel cowhands, and her gait picked up as she hurried on to enter the Emerald Bar.

The Kid didn't pay her much mind. His eyes were drawn to the hulky man lifting a buggy wheel onto a greased axle. A couple of yonkers were doing straw boss duties perched on the front buggy seat. Reining up, LaDuke gave an upward glance to the sign, which read Johanssen & Sons, then looked again at the liveryman, whose sons were carbon copies of him, with soulful blue eyes and mustard-colored hair.

"Those kids, Wiley, are 'bout's helpful as tits on a shorthorn bull. Bet there's four more like 'em at home doin' nipple-suckin' duties. Hey, you, hostler, you got hosses to swap?"

The Swede turned big gullible eyes to the newcomers. He was big-chested too, he had muscled arms big as the trunks of most limber pines, and he was hatless. "Ya, ay ban sell horses. Out back, in my corral."

The Kid, riding in closer to get into shadow, swung down. He looked about at the orderly picket of streets and tidy buildings, and it pleased him. He felt secure here, even though he'd learned of Cataldo having a town marshal. The railroad hadn't reached here either, just wagon trains and the stagecoach connecting this town to the outside world. Deeper in Idaho there'd be other places like this, but he was tired of forking a horse.

"No sense beatin' around the bush," he said. "Our hosses are worn out. Hey, you yonkers" — he poked around in a jeans pocket to pull out a couple of tinny dimes — "how'd you like some spendin' money?" He grinned as they spilled out of the buggy to come over. "One of you, beeline over to that hotel and tell 'em I want their best room. And you, up-street there's this haberdashery just about to close, I reckon. Tell 'em a couple of gents are comin' in to spend fifty or so Yankee dollars." He slipped the dimes into eager hands to have the yonkers dart away.

They merely brought their horses into stalls without bothering to unsaddle them, and went out the back door after the liveryman, and the Kid was mindful of the money stuffed into his saddlebag, which he didn't bother taking along. In the corral a dozen horses stood facing away from the lowering sun. Right away LaDuke discarded seven horses as being unfit for the trail. It came down to a grulla and an ugly hammerhead, and he said, "Guess it'll be that grulla."

Wiley Sheldon had ducked through the rails and had caught the bridle worn by a roan mare. "Reminds me of a Texas hoss I had."

"Johanssen," grinned LaDuke, "I won't beat around haggling you out of a fair price, as I'm cravin' a hot bath and a heapin' of whiskey. Fifty for both hosses and we'll throw in ours."

"That's a steal," threw in Sheldon.

"Ay ban thinking you've got a deal, mister."

Back in the livery stable, the deal was made as LaDuke handed the liveryman some folding money. He threw in another couple of dollars. "Switch our saddles to them hosses we just bought. As we could be ridin' out tonight."

When they were crossing toward the hotel, Kid LaDuke was mindful of Bonner's daughter tied out there by the river. Later on, when night had settled in, and if he wasn't too drunk to set a horse, he aimed to head out there. She always did have a mean mouth, he mused, always looked down on him. Maybe that had been part of why he'd taken her along.

But tonight's her last sunset.

About a mile out of Cataldo Rick McPherson picked up on the faint yowl of some tomcats fighting over territorial rights. With the others he took in the spread of the town by silhouetted roofs and light coming out of windows. Moonbeams piercing down at the road guided them along it, showing where that small herd of cattle had been driven from the road toward holding pens just off southwesterly.

Out front, Bonner Hudson came in further to pass a log house. The road was an arrow shaft pointing in to the main business street. He'd picked Elroy Hattan to ride in with. The rest split into pairs and waited a little before coming in to find a nighting place. When Hattan came up, the pair of them picked up to a jog, with Bonner saying, "Late as it is the bars'll still be open."

Nodding, Hattan said, "I've bet I've lost ten pounds." He eased his position somewhat on the saddle by grabbing at the saddle horn. "Lordy, any trip I take from here on will be by stagecoach."

"When we check into a hotel, Elroy, I want you to stay there. Not that we can't use an extra gun."

"I suppose I would be in the way in a gunfight."

"Chances are too, they aren't here." This was said to assuage Elroy Hattan's pride, as in Bonner was this grim expectancy. A lifetime of tracking gave a man insight into just how close he was to his prey, an unexplainable sensation gripping at him at the moment.

Back when he'd last chatted with Deputy Sheriff Jim Bob Benham, their discussion had been about those two cowhands, Cafferty and Dubay. Voicing that Cafferty was a reformed outlaw, Bonner had held back from Jim Bob the rest of what he'd been thinking. He suspected that Dancy Stuart was behind the cowhands' return. Perhaps to see that Dancy got his money back.

Dancy had shown the white feather by taking off with his racehorse. Out here that could pretty much ruin a man's reputation. This would be rankling to Dancy, so much so that he'd see to it none of them ever got back home again. Bonner hated to believe this . . . but Dancy had that reputation to protect.

Upon coming in more to the downtown sector, they found it was a spreading of four streets tied in by cross streets and alleyways, going mostly east to west to follow the flow of the main road. As he'd told the others, Bonner would check into the first hotel he sighted and the rest would find

170

rooms at other lodging places. From past experience he knew a bunch coming in together attracted a lot of attention. He took in the Spaniard Hotel issuing light from the lobby and upper rooms.

"Must be some Mex owns it."

"Could be, Elroy. If so, I've found they're more hospitable than most." He let his eyes stray opposite to the Johanssen & Sons livery stable, and would have headed there had not Hattan nudged his arm.

"Down that side street; seems to me there's light showing in that stable." Grimacing, Elroy Hattan added, "Oh, to get this backside of mine soakin' in a hot tub."

Upon stabling their horses, they strode back to the main street, and just before entering the Spaniard Hotel, Bonner took in the appearance of McPherson and Benham further east along the street. Then he was striding into the lobby as up by the desk Elroy Hattan was scrawling his name in the register book. The elderly clerk hitched his suspenders over knobby shoulder blades and made a vague attempt at brushing back a fringe of graying hair while taking in the tired set to Bonner's face.

"A hot bath," he said to Hattan in a wheezing voice of protest, "at this time of night."

Elroy Hattan dug out a silver dollar and slapped it down hard on the register book. "A hot bath, dammit. As I'm aching all over."

"A hot bath," the night clerk agreed to Bonner,

171

who smiled as he picked up the quilled pen. He turned to watch Hattan laboring up the staircase before tending to the business of signing in, and he made quiet inquiry if a party of two men and a young woman had checked into the hotel within the last few hours.

"Nope, mister, they come and go."

"This is important," said Bonner as he removed from an inner coat pocket a couple of Reward posters. Though crumbled and faded, the images of the outlaws Kid LaDuke and his sidekick, Sheldon, were still vivid. "This one, this is Kid LaDuke. Read his description . . . short and thin and packing two six-guns."

"Yeah, come to think on it, a couple of strangers checked in earlier tonight. I was told this by the other clerk . . . ah, here's there names."

"Just the two of them?"

"You did mention a woman? Got the key to room 212 if you want to check it out. Say, are you a lawman?"

"Out of Montana." Bonner palmed the key and added, "I'd keep this under your hat if they come back."

"I'll do that, but like I said, I wasn't here when they checked in." The night clerk watched the tall stranger head upstairs, then, still grumbling, he reclaimed his rocking chair.

From the deep silence coming out of the room Bonner realized it was empty. Then he let himself in, and eased the door shut. The room contained two narrow beds and other furniture. Strewn

172

about was clothing, and on the only table reposed one saddlebag over another. One saddlebag had an assortment of items useful to the trail, and he found the other had been emptied out. He stood there in the quiet darkness of the room and sorted out what to do next.

"Could be the Kid and the other one? But again, where's Lily—"

Just as he turned to head out of the room, his boot shoved something on the floor into wavy motion, and bending he picked up a twenty-dollar bill. "Not too many drifters have bills this large. The Kid? Got to think it's him."

Outside in the hallway he locked the door before hurrying to the room they'd rented for the night. There he found Elroy Hattan stripped down to his red flannels. He showed Hattan the money he'd come across, and said,

"After you take that bath, Elroy, I'd stick close to this room. Found this just down the hall in room 212; could be where the Kid's staying. If it's him."

"You goin' looking for 'em in the bars, I reckon."

"Yup. And Elroy, they know you from back at Salt Creek. Sightin' you could spook them out of here."

"Don't worry, Bonner, I'll stick here until you get back. An' you just might still find me soakin' in that tub next door. What about Lily?"

Just for a moment Bonner Hudson shared the anxiety he saw etched on Hattan's face. Then

173

with a curt nod he was gone.

Out in front of the hotel, he held under the shadowing porch, going over what they'd planned. He could rely on Jim Bob and McPherson, but the unknown quantity were the pair of cowhands. Frank Cafferty was an easy man to like, but again there was the man's checkered past. And Lem Dubay just seemed to be Cafferty's shadow. The plan was if anyone sighted the hardcases to come back to the first bar they sighted when pulling into Cataldo, in this case the Emerald Bar. That money of Dancy's, now being spent by the Kid, would hold him here. Bonner had the notion those hardcases would give up once they were together and they realized they were outnumbered.

But the Kid . . . just might decide to unlimber his guns . . . as he's unpredictable as the weather hereabouts.

The cowhands didn't bother leaving their horses at a livery stable but pulled them in behind a small rooming house on the western outskirts of Cataldo. What drew them in was a big white sign behind a picket fence fronting a two-story house. Lights were still showing on both floors, so they rode around back, with Frank Cafferty going over and rapping on the screen door.

A young girl appeared, and when Cafferty asked about a room, she went scampering off to bring back her mother. As he stood there, Cafferty wasn't sure if they'd be in need of a room. For if they came across Kid LaDuke, it was Cafferty's intentions to divest the outlaw of that money, and then pull out tonight.

He wouldn't be here at all if it hadn't of been for Dancy Stuart. Back there on the trail the rancher had pulled him aside, him and Dubay, and pitched this deal about going back to join up with the posse. Dancy had been damned certain Bonner Hudson was going to catch up to Kid La-Duke. Then all of that money Dancy had paid to get his precious racehorse back would be Cafferty and Lem Dubay's if nobody came back to tell of Dancy's cowardice.

Mused Frank Cafferty, just working for rancher Dancy Stuart would build up a hate for the man, he was so damned arrogant and rich. *Why is it men like him get rich? Just bigger thieves is all I can figure.*

Along the way here Frank Cafferty had been brooding over just how to handle this. They concluded that just taking out the Kid would be enough. As punishment for Dancy Stuart would be Bonner and everyone else returning to the Flathead Valley and setting the record straight.

Now he smiled at a matronly woman sweeping into the kitchen, and Cafferty made inquiry about a room.

"I see there are two of you?"

"Just the lonesome pair of us. An' just for tonight, I'm hopin'."

"Would two dollars be too much . . ."

"Ma'am, that's more'n fair. That shed out back; like to leave our horses there."

"Yes, you might find some sweet feed sacked up too."

They left within the half hour to walk down a lane lined by elm trees, where Dubay said, "Glad you decided not to do what Dancy wants."

"Dancy screwed up, plain and simple. An' Bonner ain't the man to forget, nor forgive. Forty thousand split two ways is more money either of us has ever seen."

"I hear the Kid is fast as they come."

"One thing he don't have is eyes in the back of his head. If the sonofabitch is here, he's celebrating, and drink'll slow any man down. Besides, Lem, he's spending our money."

Chapter Sixteen

Over at Hickey's Haberdashery a bright red shirt cut Western style had caught the Kid's eye. So it wouldn't do but he had to have that shirt and other clothing to match up to it, a black leather vest and black wristbands and black boots embossed with a fancy design. Under the new Stetson his hair was slicked back. He reeked of pomade, mothballs, and naphtha. He felt damned good about himself as him and Wiley Sheldon set out to wreak havoc upon the night spots of Cataldo.

"You can spot that shirt a mile away, Kid."

"I don't aim for them to get that close."

"Yippeee!"

He grinned at Sheldon ogling a woman framed in the front window of a saloon. As Sheldon picked up his pace as they began crossing over, Kid LaDuke reached up to caress the wide brim of his new hat, then he settled it more to the right. "There ain't nobody in town packin' as much cash as us," he exulted silently. For under the gunbelt there was a new money belt containing the bulk of the reward money. The wallet bulging out a back Levi pocket was thick with greenbacks too, as he'd discarded the notion of leaving any money in the hotel safe. Teddy LaDuke didn't trust strongboxes and banks.

The Golden Nugget was the first saloon they hit, buying drinks around to get the feel of spending money. With two fingers hooked around the shot glass, the Kid muttered happily, "They call it the aqua vitae of the West."

"Oh, Mr. LaDuke, you're so handsome."

He grinned his love of the moment for the whore at his side, even though threads of gray hair poked through the red henna a shade duller than the Kid's shirt. Hell, he basked in her adulation. So too was Wiley Sheldon making no effort to ward off the furtive hand of the woman he was with coming to rest on his inner thigh. "What's yer name, ma'am?"

"Sugah, it's Catherine Duveriux."

"Like hell," laughed Sheldon.

"Now would I lie to you, sugah."

"Just like you wouldn't tell no untruths to your grandchildren—"

"Why you . . . son'bitch!" She made a grab for his stein of beer to have something to throw at the hardcase lurching up from the chair, but he yanked it away. "Kid, we've worn out our welcome, I reckon."

Laughing, the Kid said, "Wiley, you've got a smart mouth. But what the hell"—he let some paper money flutter onto the bar top—"let's vamoose, as this 'pears to be a rest home for the infirm and aged."

The half-filled pitcher of beer Wiley Sheldon had left back on the table struck the swinging batwing, spilling glass and beer, after the hardcases ducking along the boardwalk. "I can tell," chortled Sheldon, "this is gonna be the start of one beautful night. You know, Kid, I think the one you were with likes you. We could . . ."

"I ain't ready to be rocked to sleep, partner. Shoulda bought some cigars."

Under a velvety black sky they cut onto other streets in pursuit of means to fulfill their lusts, for Sheldon a chance to show off to the whores he was flush, the Kid trying to live up to his brag as being a connoisseur of his favorite aqua vitae. A couple of hours into his drinking bout, that ugly mood of Kid LaDuke's began surfacing. His prey was a man braced up by crutches at the front end of the bar.

First LaDuke turned to see how his drinking companion was faring over at a nearby table. Sheldon had one arm draped over the shoulders of one whore while two more were laughing at something he'd just said, but mostly ogling the greenbacks spread out before the hardcase. Now they laughed at their table mate trying to refill their shot glasses, the whiskey dribbling onto the green-felt tabletop.

"You'd better let me pour, honey."

"Man can't pour whiskey," he slurred out, "man

179

shouldn't be drinking. There, some for you gals, some for me."

Kid LaDuke got to looking at one of the whores, as she appeared to be no older'n him, but gussied up in so much paint it was hard to tell exactly. Unlike the other two she was deep-chested, he couldn't help noticing, and then the man propped up by crutches called out in that wheezing voice of his for another drink. This triggered something in the Kid, and he spun that way, and clearing leather.

"Damn, you sound like a preacher I once knew. Down in Nevada. Like you was tryin' to preach to us now, dammit." He pulled the trigger to have the leaden slug follow the downward tilt of the barrel and bust into the man's wooden crutch to shatter the lower end away.

Somehow the man kept from falling by clutching at the bar, and grimacing, as his right leg was encased in plaster up to his kneecap. "Please, can't you see I . . ."

"Dance, preacher! Dammit — dance!"

Bammity-Bam-Bam!

He screamed as one of the slugs penetrated into his left hip, and fell heavily, and the Kid busted out laughing. "Anybody else care to dance!" There was a challenge in his voice; if anybody in the smoky confines of this dingy saloon wanted some of the same, the Kid would damn well oblige. "Chickenshits . . ." came the Kid's grumbling voice as he realized Wiley Sheldon had come up to him.

"Come on, Kid, you've pissed everybody off.

180

Got this woman for ya. Here, Mimi, say howdy to my partner."

LaDuke, focusing in on her face, saw it was the one he'd been admiring, and he grinned away his anger. But for good measure, and to add insult to injury, he spun to fan a couple of slugs out at the long mirror behind the back bar. Then he really got ugly when he chanced to spot one of the bartenders dipping an arm down to pick up a greener.

"Don't kill him, Kid."

Somehow Sheldon's interfering at that moment held the Kid's fire. He dipped the barrel of his six-gun upward and said loud for all to hear, "Here, here's a hundred bucks; chickenshits."

It was Wiley Sheldon backing out after the others, and when he got outside to join up with the three whores and his partner, hubbub and music flowed out of the saloon they'd just vacated.

From here it was an hour of bar-hopping before Kid LaDuke was brought around a dark corner by the whore with him, where she pointed at a large building set in the center of the block.

"Shanahan's Golden Nugget Casino. I'm going to ask for a job there next week."

"That so." The Kid in trying to match his stride to hers caught a boot heel on the uneven planking and tripped forward, and she clutched at his arm. Then he was sweeping her in close, one arm around her bare shoulders, the other hand groping at her buttocks, and with her wiggling in closer.

"Hey, Kid, there's an alley—"

"Poker!" said LaDuke. "Gonna clean me some clocks."

"Then come on," Wiley Sheldon said to the whores clinging to his arms.

It seemed unusual to Frank Cafferty the taverns being so lively until he realized it was Saturday night. Busting around the corner they were ambling toward were a handful of cowhands astride their broncs. They spilled off their horses by the hitching rack to walk thirstily into the Elk Bar, which provoked from Cafferty's sidekick a grin.

"I've had the same thirst. Still get the urge."

Cafferty said, "As I recollect so does Teddy La-Duke. He was born a hell-raiser. If he's here, it'll be him holed up in some saloon."

In passing, Lem Dubay took a gander at the Flying M brand etched on each bronc. Then he caught up to Frank Cafferty peering in through the batwings. The last time either of them had run into Kid LaDuke was at least five years ago, and before that had been brief encounters in Flathead Valley towns, with Cafferty doubtful as to the Kid remembering them. He grimaced as there was no sign of LaDuke and the other hardcase, or of Bonner's daughter.

"He wouldn't take her to the bars, Bonner's kid. If she's still alive, which is doubtful, he'll probably have her hog-tied in his room. Can't help musing on that incident at Lone Tree."

"Him raping those girls before doin' murder. My feelin' is she's dead, this Lily."

182

"Well, these boots ain't made for traipsin'."

"My turn to buy." Dubay shouldered past his companion and into the saloon. The tables were full, so he swung in toward the bar built with the front half coming toward the front windows and angling back along a side wall. There were a few incurious glances thrown at the newcomers wedging a place at the bar.

After they'd gotten drinks, Cafferty said, "This town ain't a bad place to be on Sat'day night; things don't work out maybe a spread around here'll be hirin'."

"Maybe," grunted Lem Dubay as he stood there taking in a conversation coming from a nearby table. "You catch that?"

One of those seated at the table was in the midst of telling how a couple of strangers had come into his haberdashery shop. "Business hasn't been all that good. But these two gents come in packing a wad of greenbacks. Sure a grubby pair. But what they spent comes to about a week's profit."

"The Kid."

"Got to be," echoed Dubay.

"Takes a load off my mind."

From the table, "This one, cowhand you'd call him, just had to have this bright red shirt. You know, Ben, the one I had in my display window."

"Lucky one of my bulls didn't see it," laughed the cattleman. "Then it woulda been me payin' for a new front window and that godawful red shirt."

The pair seeking Kid LaDuke pulled away from

the bar to create no further stir of interest when they left the saloon. Bolstered by what they'd heard, they took the time to hold at the corner and decide where to head next. Dubay reached for the makings, a nervous tension building in him.

He said, "The question is, Frank, will he have that money with him . . ."

"Most likely he will. As the Kid don't put money into banks but takes it out." He grinned at his joke in an attempt to make light of what was coming up. For he knew that Dubay's only use for a gun had been to kill some predator or use the butt to drive a nail into a fence post. "I don't know how late these bars stay open; most likely around three o'clock. Or some all night. That gambling hall we was told about—"

"What was it, Shanahan's?" Dubay got his tailor-made going and sucked in smoke.

Over on the next street Kid LaDuke motioned to the blackjack dealer he wanted a hit. He had a trey showing, the Kid's hole card a nine of hearts. A brown-paper handrolled dangled from his mouth, which opened to say, "Hold that card." He slid out a blue chip to double his bet as ash dropped from his cigarette onto his new shirt.

The dealer shook his head around a skeptical smile. "Your poison, mister." He pulled the top card out of the box, a five. "You've got eight showing."

"Tell you what," muttered the Kid. "I feel lucky. I'm betting forty I don't bust. Another forty says I hit twenty-one right on the head."

His smile holding, the dealer waited until the man in the red shirt added more chips to what he'd already wagered.

The girl clutching at LaDuke's shoulder asked, "Am I your lucky charm . . ."

"Here's to your health," he said to her as he flipped the contents of the shot glass into his mouth.

"A hundred you don't hit," another player said to the Kid, whereupon Kid LaDuke nodded it was a bet.

Quickly the dealer skimmed out the next card, and when he flipped it over in front of LaDuke it proved out to be the four of clubs. LaDuke just stood there looking at the card, then he gestured to Wiley Sheldon to refill his shot glass. "Well, did I or didn't I?" He held the grimace as the dealer dealt to fill out the hands of the other players. The dealer held at nineteen.

He pierced LaDuke with anxious eyes.

"Anybody want to bet my hole card is a nine—"

Uncertainty stabbed at everyone in the game and the blackjack dealer.

The man who'd bet the hundred was a rancher in to sell some cattle, and he had, and he said loudly, "Come on, turn over that hole card as I figure you busted."

The Kid spun out a six-shooter and laid it on his cards, a wicked grin directed at the rancher. "So then I owe you a hundred." Now he shoved what chips he had left out into the middle of the

185

blackjack table. "Around three hundred there. You willing to cover that?"

"Dammit, no!" snapped the rancher, only to have a man who was standing at the end of the table taking in the game speak out as he reached in to remove his wallet from an inner coat pocket.

"You're kind of whiskeyed up," he said not unkindly, "and a man's luck can hold only so long. Here, my three hundred says your hole card isn't a nine."

Picking up his six-gun, Kid LaDuke turned his hole card over, with the dealer merely grunting in disgust. LaDuke couldn't keep from laughing as he reached over to get the paper money he'd won. "Drinks for the house."

No sooner had the rancher and another player quit the game than others claimed their places. The music seemed to pick up louder, while at the table Wiley Sheldon had just made his pitch to one of the whores. She seemed more'n eager to leave to find a room, but the other girl there suddenly stiffened in her chair, with her eyes widening, a look that Sheldon knew meant trouble. He twisted in his chair for a quick look over his shoulder, and when he saw the one man there holding a gun, he cried out, "Kid!"

At the same time the hardcase tried rising from the chair as he clawed for his handgun. Sheldon got it out, but, then he felt a leaden slug hammering into his belly, and one more that took him just below the mouth. He fell hard, with the two girls still frozen to their chairs, as the sound

186

of Lem Dubay's guns was answered by the Kid's.

Dubay staggered backward and took two more hits from LaDuke's hammering gun before LaDuke felt a slug nip past his right arm and realized there were two of them. A snarl of desperation busting from the Kid, he reached out to pull the whore in front of him. Coming in through the batwings, Frank Cafferty knew that Dubay should have held his fire, but it was too late for that now. His first slug barely missing, Cafferty thumbed the hammer back on his six-gun to trigger a bullet from it that struck into the woman.

Kid LaDuke opened up.

The slugs struck within the span of a silver dollar into the center of Cafferty's chest. A look of surprise gaped open his eyes as he muttered, "Kid . . . you damn coward . . ."

Now the cowhand pitched forward to rattle dead against the floorboards, and with the Kid pulling away from the woman he let slump down by the blackjack table, the Kid, all wild-eyed, letting go with a nervous laugh.

"You seen it!" he shouted with the heavier report of gunfire still ringing out in the heavy silence. "They shot my partner in the back!"

Nobody noticed the batwings being brushed open until the man who'd entered said, "Been a long haul, Teddy."

"Bonner Hudson?" Somehow he kept from firing when he realized Bonner hadn't drawn his six-gun. "Yup, you played hell catching up, I hear."

"Lily . . ."

"Yeah, your precious Lily." He looked around, but it seemed everyone was rooted to their chairs or just standing there, as they knew this wasn't over. As for the Kid, he enjoyed the sudden limelight. If his name hadn't counted for much out in these parts before, it sure as hell would now.

"Just passing through your town," he announced, keeping his eyes glued to the tracker. "Name's Kid LaDuke. And this hombre, calls himself a tracker."

"Is she still alive?" Bonner asked calmly, though inside he was struggling to control his anger.

"Lily? You any good with that hogiron, Mr. Hudson?" He leathered his right gun.

This was going to end in bloodshed, Bonner knew. Teddy LaDuke wasn't about to give up his guns. Drained inside from his fears about his daughter, he took in the mocking smile on a face he'd learned to hate. "Folks, I'm packing a badge. This man kidnapped my daughter. Has got a lot of blood on his hands. Yup, LaDuke, I'll oblige you."

"Then, Bonner, you'll never find out what happened to her . . . as you'll be dead . . ." Confidentially the Kid went for his left gun, and it came out faster than Bonner's. In his haste to kill, instead of penetrating into the chest the slug struck into Bonner's side, spinning him out of the way of another slug. Through the Kid's flung-out curse Bonner triggered his weapon as he bounced into the bar vacated moments ago.

The Kid sagged down on buckling knees, but

somehow he held on his feet, yelling, "That bitch of a daughter of yours . . . she's dead, Bonner . . . she's dead . . ." In rapid succession he took two more hits. The Kid fired too, but wildly. Then he was slumping down, bleeding, busted up inside, and dying.

Clutching at his side, Bonner hurried over. He knelt down and turned Teddy LaDuke over onto his belly to gaze into LaDuke's eyes beginning to glaze over. "Where is she, Teddy?"

The Kid coughed up blood and a babble of words, "Me . . . and Lily'll . . . be waltzing in . . . hell . . ." A chortling kind of laugh came from the outlaw as he plunged into a deep blackness.

An anguish so deep it penetrated into bone overtook Bonner Hudson. He rose, and for now all he could do was stare down at LaDuke. A chair scraped behind him, there was a whisper, then movement came again to the gambling casino, and one of the bartenders asked someone to go and fetch the town marshal.

"Mister."

"Ah, yes?"

"I saw them ride in. It was just the two of them."

Bonner nodded around the pain he felt.

"That was somethin', though. That gunfight. Never seen the like before."

But Bonner had moved away, and they watched Bonner Hudson shove outside and head out along the dusky street of a night about half over.

Chapter Seventeen

The last time gunfire had been heard in Cataldo was back a couple of years, and that time it was just a drunken cowboy emptying the loads of his six-gun skyward. A few late drinkers came out of saloons as Bonner Hudson turned a corner to let the lights from Shanahan's Golden Nugget Casino fade away. This wasn't the first time he'd known the sting of a bullet, but all the same one never got used to being hit.

"Hey," a man called out from the boardwalk to Bonner striding up the middle of the street, "what's goin' on?"

"Dunno," responded Bonner without looking. Coming onto the next corner, he slowed as deputies Benham and McPherson came into view. He pulled in to a side wall and shrugged out of his coat. The deputies pulled in by him, and he probed with his fingers at the wound. "Slug passed through."

"The Kid?"

"Dead. So are three more."

"We heard some guns hammering away."

Bonner said, "They checked into the Spaniard Hotel; same's us. But they didn't bring Lily along."

"They had to stable their hosses; maybe they left her there."

"Maybe. An' I figure that'll be that stable just across the street. Rick, you'd better roust Elroy Hattan—a room on the second floor. We'll be at that stable."

As Rick McPherson broke out ahead, Bonner and Jim Bob headed the same way, with questions dancing in Jim Bob's eyes. And he said, "You said three more . . ."

"Cafferty and Dubay went down, that sidekick of the Kid's. And Dancy's money? I expect they'll find the money on LaDuke." Bonner grimaced as his boot found a chuckhole.

He looked away from Benham to the midnight sky. Through the streets a chill had come down from the higher reaches of the mountains. Like the Kid said, his daughter could be dead. But he had to be sure, and that meant tracking out from the stable and eastward along the stagecoach road. For if they hadn't brought Lily into Cataldo, she'd be out there, which in all probability meant someplace along the river.

Inside the stable, Benham took a lantern down from a wall peg. He struck a lucifer into flame against a nearby post and got the lantern going. The wooden match he dropped down at his feet and pressed firmly into the hard dirt floor. Bonner went on ahead and called back that he'd found two horses saddled and ready to be ridden out. He brought back the horse the Kid had bought and said to Jim Bob, "You'd better saddle two more horses. I'll keep along the road until I find fresh tracks."

"Be awful hard, Bonner, picking up on any tracks tonight."

"I know, but I got no choice."

Draping his coat over the saddle, Bonner pulled up his shirt to examine the wound, which was swollen some and purpled. *Had worse,* he mused, *and besides, the pain of this can't compare to what I'll feel if the Kid wasn't lying.* Glancing at Jim Bob as he put on his coat, he said, "It could be they had intentions of heading north through that gap back there. If so, they might have crossed the river."

Nodding, Benham speculated, "Then recrossed it to come here."

Once he was saddlebound, a nudge from Bonner's spurs brought the bronc out of the stable and loping to the east. He held it to this gait until he was past the holding pens and the last buildings of Cataldo. Still he rode on in the inky cloak of night, but at a slower gait. Now that his eyes had gotten accustomed to the settled fabric of darkness, he could make out objects he'd missed before. Under starlight he could see the pale glint of water standing in low places marked by reeds and patches of brush. He cut northerly and then out about fifty rods he veered into a searching route paralleling the road. Unlike before when he had to cross that river swollen by rain, Bonner was grateful for the softer ground he was riding over.

Reining up, he took in where an elk had just passed through by the few hoofprints he found. "An old-timer," he determined.

Then he pressed on in the fullness of night as out of Cataldo came the rest of those looking for Bonner's daughter.

The tracks Bonner had picked up on brought him down onto the floodplain of the Coeur d'Alene. Got to be them, for it didn't make any sense anyone crossing this section of the river when the main crossing lay further to the east. He'd come across the tracks about a mile out of Cataldo, and now he found they ended in a muddy explosion at the water's edge.

Dragging out his six-gun, he triggered it once, to fetch in the others, and in the hopes too if Lily was out here someplace, it would bring her cry for help.

As he holstered his gun, he judged the river to be up some. Shouldn't be any problem fording it. He would have shaped a hand-rolled, but the worry of the moment was about more than he could bear. He kept keening his ears to the vague night sounds. He sank within himself to let the valley begin speaking to him, as most sounds coming through here were muted to the singing of trees or wind humming through buffalo grass. The lonely call of a loon sent an expectant shiver coursing in to tell the tracker he wasn't alone, the yip-yapping of a coyote coming out of the far distance.

Sensing the presence of the others, Bonner swung the bronc away from the river, and there the three riders were, breaking down a cutbank to come loping onto the floodplain and to vanish in the lower scattering of ragged brush and trees. The bronc whickered a greeting to Rick McPherson reining in first.

"We picked up on their tracks too."

"If it's them . . ."

"Yonder," said Bonner, "is that gap and maybe the Kid's original intentions to head up thataway. Just two riders crossing here tell me she's still out there."

Elroy Hattan, bundled up in his coat, said, "Can't believe how cold it can get out here at night."

"Be hard on her," said Jim Bob. "Just get this feeling she's still alive. So . . ."

"Yup," agreed Bonner, "once we cross over, we'll fan out, and you see that cut up to that high plateau; I figure they came down through it."

"How you faring?"

"That slug passed through, so I won't die from lead poisoning."

Then Bonner was urging his horse down the wide riverbank and into the sluggish waters. The first part of the crossing went well as it was shallow, but with an impish suddenness the river deepened, and everyone settled deeper in their saddles to let their mounts swim with the angling current tugging at them.

Once they were coming onto the far bank, Bonner brought them westerly.

She awoke to the cold and the confusion of the moment and tried rising, only to have the painful reality of the ropes binding her bring a sob tearing from her lips. What Lily Hudson knew she'd heard was a single gunshot. Now her fear was that Teddy LaDuke was on his way back.

"Damn him," she cried out.

The cowhand's soogans had pulled away from her body, and it came to her now just how cold she was, as shivers lanced up her arms. "Why," Lily called out, "didn't he just kill me," and as she kicked out with her legs in an attempt to drag in the worn quilt.

Brush crackling nearby sent terror in to embrace Lily. There came the realization this was bear country, or it could be a mountain lion in search of prey, or a dreaded wolverine.

An agonizing snarl of anger shattered the frozen silence, and Lily espied a shape blacker than the night suddenly come busting out of the underbrush, and she screamed her fear at a huge silvertip lurching in to where she lay tied to the dead tree. The grizzly picked up on her fear, for it suddenly slowed down and lumbered up to stand on

195

its hind legs. On it came, its piggish eyes red-rimmed and sighting in on its vilest enemy.

All Lily could see were those eyes, the dull gleam of those fangs in the gaping mouth, and the talons hooked to those massive paws, and she screamed again and shrank away from this specter of death.

Another voice added its sound to the snarling fury of the silvertip, the deep-throated roar of a Winchester in a rapid fusillade.

Drawn in by her screams, Rick McPherson had dismounted at a gallop and began throwing slugs at the enraged grizzly. It caused the grizzly to spin away from the tree, confused and drawn to the two-legged creature a scant ten yards away.

"Come on!" McPherson yelled. "Come on! That's it." He kept working the lever on his rifle and firing even as the grizzly started at him though mortally wounded.

Somehow he evaded that first weakened charge and the outsweeping forepaw that, had it struck him, would have torn his scalp away.

"Come on, damn you!"

He scored hits in the midsection and took out one of the silvertip's eyes. But it was turning and still seeking him when his rifle jammed. Without hesitating the young lawman palmed his six-gun and began backing toward Lily and pumping away at the grizzly. He could scarcely believe it when the silvertip seemed to waver before crumbling down, and he held his fire.

Now he spun around and went in to drop down

by Lily Hudson, who was wracked with tears. All he could think to do was to take her in his arms as her incoherent words came to him, and he blurted out, "Oh, Lily, we've found you . . . how I love you . . ."

Suddenly it came to Deputy Sheriff Rick McPherson that she'd gone limp in his arms, and of what he'd just said, and of the thud of hooves as the others came in. He jerked up some when a rifle sounded.

Twisting to look, he realized it had been Bonner letting go at the silvertip, which was just starting to rise again. He fumbled out his pocketknife as Bonner swung down to nudge the barrel of his rifle at the bear's head. Then he cut the ropes away from Lily's wrists and legs as Bonner came in to gaze down at his daughter.

"She . . . she 'pears to be okay . . ."

"She's alive, is all that matters."

"I—I'll get a fire going." But he held to peel out of his sheepskin. "She'll need this."

From Bonner there was an appreciative nod, and then he was spreading out the soogans and lifting Lily onto it. He draped the sheepskin around her gaunt frame, leaned closer to kiss his daughter on the cheek even as he took in the marks on her face. "Lily . . ." He brushed a teardrop away from her closed eye, fought back his own tears.

Their horses tethered downwind to keep them from picking up the smell of the dead grizzly, and clustered around a large campfire, the presence of Lily Hudson brought forth smiles. She hadn't come around, which brought Bonner glancing at his daughter.

"Here," said Jim Bob, "this'll warm your innards."

"Already had my share."

"A little more won't hurt. As it's over, Bonner."

"I reckon so," he agreed, but there was still his concern about the long trip home. And there was Dancy Stuart. Those cowhands of Dancy's were dead now, but it still lay heavy in Bonner's mind that the reward money was only part of it. But he gazed now at Lily with the realization she needed a doctor's care, as he did. And a warm bed after all those cold nights on the trail.

"She's resting more comfortably," he murmured, more for his own benefit than for the others. "But we'll pull out soon's she comes around."

Chapter Eighteen

This time the lowering sun was at their backs as they traversed the valley floor. Instead of the wariness of before, smiles were etched on their faces, as deputy sheriffs McPherson and Benham, and Elroy Hattan, took in the hump of land where they'd had that firefight with the outlaws.

"Ancient history now," said Jim Bob.

"Reckon so. I wonder if Grisham made it back to Big Rock."

"It'll be a sad homecoming," he said to Rick McPherson, and by now Jim Bob knew the man they worked for had been laid to rest. "Harv Black, he sure took it personal, this thing between him and Kid LaDuke. Just got this feeling the sheriff expected to die up there." His glance swung eastward to the high gap in the mountains marking Lookout Pass.

"What about you, Mr. Hattan, I expect you'll be glad to see Salt Creek again?"

The few days they'd lingered back at Cataldo

had allowed some saddle sores to heal. And for various reasons all of them had accompanied the hearse and another wagon bearing those killed in that gunfight at Shanahan's Golden Nugget Casino. There'd been no church services, and at the bone orchard (as Jim Bob had called it) and after the crude pine boxes had been lowered into the ground, everyone had looked to Bonner Hudson for his final opinion. They hadn't been expecting any words of grace.

But the tracker had fooled them as he'd gazed about, to the town marshal and undertaker, the few locals. Then he'd doffed his Stetson.

"Teddy LaDuke . . . the others, you might say died by the sword according to what I've read in the Book of Leviticus. They shall fall one upon another . . . as it were before a sword . . ."

Now with the wind ruffling out of the northwest, Deputy Sheriff Benham looked ahead to Bonner and his daughter riding side by side. Every once in a while Lily would reach out to touch her father's arm—a comforting gesture. Benham reckoned this made up for a lot of things.

Stuffed in Bonner's saddlebags was the shank of that reward money. Though back at Cataldo he felt it only proper to use some of it to pay for the burial expenses, and what the doctor charged to tend to him and Lily. Then it was their lodging and meals as they'd lingered on for a couple of days to rest up for the long ride home.

Bonner could tell that Lily was a changed woman. There had been a moment of quiet relief when she'd come flat out to say that neither La-Duke nor any other outlaw had molested her, not that this hadn't been in the Kid's plans. Her inquiries about Kelsay Stuart had elicited from Bonner the true character of the man she intended to marry. She still had Kelsay's ring, but she thrust it in a saddlebag. In her mind he had branded himself a coward, and ever since she'd known the truth, Lily was beginning to realize she'd been bedazzled by all that he could offer her.

Back of her rode a young man she'd spurned. In the terror of the moment, he'd been there to take out that grizzly. She couldn't shake from her thoughts and dreams just how horrible it had been, not only the attack by the bear, but all that Teddy LaDuke had done to her.

Rick, she mused inwardly, *did I hear him right back there? About loving me?* A few miles ahead lay a town where they'd stay overnight, and where she was determined to confront Rick McPherson.

Concern for her father brought Lily Hudson's eyes that way in a guarded glance. He may have shielded it from the others, but Lily could sense when Bonner was troubled. She could read the body signs he sent out. Did he really believe Kelsay's father might be lurking up there, waiting to ambush them? He hadn't voiced this to her, but it was there in the anxious set to his face.

"Dad, it is over, isn't it?"

Her question startled Bonner out of his pondering reveries, and he blinked to chase the worry away. "I'm hoping it is. But knowing Dancy . . ."

201

He grimaced, tugged his hat up, and said, "Trouble is, Dancy Stuart has got to have things his way. What rankles me, Lily, is him not givin' a damn about anything but that hoss of his. There's his pride too; got stung to the quick. Seen pride make men commit most anything—"

Lily Hudson kept looking over at where her father was having a long talk with Jim Bob Benham. The Carlton Hotel was a pleasant interlude after the rigors of sleeping outdoors. They'd pulled into Bridger a little before sundown, a small town Lily could remember passing through at night.

Her face still bore some healing scabs, though the swelling around her eyes had gone down. This had brought curious glances from the waitresses working in the modest dining room of the hotel. All the while Lily had been casting sidelong glances at Rick McPherson. The one time he'd looked into her eyes had brought a flush to his face. And there was something else which made Lily fully aware that he cared for her.

With the evening meal over, everyone had come out here onto the veranda to watch yet another day come to a close. Westerly the purpling sky was merging with the serrated peaks. While Lily sat alone as the one she knew as Hattan sat talking to Rick McPherson. Abruptly she rose from the wicker chair and went to confront the two of them.

"Mr. McPherson, we have to talk."

"I?" He shot a glance at Bonner Hudson, and then made a grab for his hat perched next to him on the long bench stashed against the front wall of the hotel. "I reckon so, Miss Lily."

Earlier she'd seen the grove of trees out behind the hotel, and this was where she brought Deputy Sheriff McPherson. She came in under a branch bowed low with the weight of green apples and gazed back at a moonbeam haloing Rick's face. Before he'd just been around Big Rock, somewhat shy and uncertain about himself. But there'd been no uncertainty about the way he'd risked his life, and though Lily had spoken to Rick about this, suddenly she was fumbling for the right words to say.

"Ah, Lily, it is a right pretty night."

She realized his voice sounded different, the chord of it deeper and a husky baritone, and now when he removed his hat, her eyes went to the thick black hair, the way the bronzed skin lay tight against his high cheekbones. "I . . . I wanted to say . . ."

"You know, we never did talk all that much . . . before."

My gosh, came a shocking thought to Lily Hudson, that it was this man she cared for. Otherwise why would she stand here all atremble, with feelings touching the secret parts of her body, and be so damned tongue-tied. Coming out from under the apple tree, she reached a nervous hand to brush a lock of hair away from her face and took

203

a tentative step to bring her deeper into the trees. Then she turned quickly, and there he was, within arm's-length. And it seemed perfectly natural to melt into his arms.

Moments later she pulled away, her cheeks flushed and kind of angry at herself, and she said, "Back there . . . just after you killed the bear . . . you took me in your arms . . ."

"My gosh," he grinned, "reckon I did."

"What was it you told me?"

This time it was Deputy Sheriff McPherson fumbling for something to say, relieved too it was a shade darker here under the trees. "Maybe . . . maybe, Miss Lily, you know how I feel about you—"

Her soft melodic laughter rang out as she regained some of her composure, knowing now what it was to really care for someone, and yet there was this bedeviling side of Lily's nature that caused her to say, "You still haven't told me what you said, exactly."

"Lily, I, I . . . I love you."

Her smile held.

"I, I can't give you all that Kelsay can. Goshdarn too, Lily, I forgot you're still engaged . . ."

"Was."

"Oh, that means . . ."

"You'll have to speak to my father."

"Ohm'gosh, Bonner."

* * *

The young man Lily was no longer engaged to was experiencing different emotions at the moment. Around Kelsay Stuart up in the high mountain pass was the cold of night, but chiefly a strange dread as sharing the remoteness of their campfire seemed to be the cold presence of men recently killed.

He took in his father skylined on rocks just about where Lookout Pass took that long plunge eastward toward Salt Creek. The man he was staring at had become a stranger. It seemed all his father could ramble on about was his lost honor, of redemption, and of just holding here to see if those who'd gone after Kid LaDuke would come back. Even the money seemed unimportant to Dancy Stuart.

Kelsay Stuart poked the stick he held at the burning wood, and sparks and ash flared up. "Damn"—he kicked a small hunk of wood deeper into the flames—"this doesn't make any sense. We've got Pa's racehorse."

And any regrets he still felt about pulling out to leave Lily Hudson at the mercy of those outlaws were buried, a thing of the past. Pa'd been right, about me just wanting to bed Lily. Now he just wanted to get back with his drinking buddies and take on a whore or two.

Snaking a glance up the pass, he saw that his father was traipsing back. But he held his eyes there as a shudder gripped his shoulders, for the unburied remains of those outlaws were still up there. He scratched at the straw-colored stubble on

205

his face as Dancy Stuart came in to squat down to his son's right.

"Pa, we could just as well have waited down at Salt Creek. Damn cold up here. We . . ."

The rancher reached out to grip his son's forearm, to say in a cold and cutting voice, "You still don't understand what's happened! Time you grew up, boy. Time you found out it's them in the valley against us Stuarts." He pulled his hand away and picked up a tin cup.

"We . . . we've got friends, Pa."

"We won't have anybody finds out how we took off. Might as well be dead that happens."

"But . . . Pa, there's that deputy sheriff; the one we seen coming into Salt Creek with the sheriff's body."

"Don't worry about Grisham. It's the others, Bonner, the rest." His jaw snapping shut. Still grasping the empty cup, he gazed into his son's eyes. For some time he held to his silence, trying to plumb the depths of Kelsay's comprehension of what they had to do. "Son, I reckon it's about time you grew up."

He plucked the blackened coffeepot out of the flames and filled his cup, their shadows fanning out to merge blackly with the night. The rancher figured he would hold here until tomorrow noon, then if nobody showed, he would head into Idaho. He was tired from the long chase after the Kid, the aftermath of it mostly. It didn't matter none now that he couldn't backtrack what he'd done, and even now he didn't consider it a matter of cowardice. But he'd be judged by others, and with all the enemies he had, well, he just couldn't allow any of them to return to the Flathead Valley.

"My will, Kelsay, says you inherit the ranch."

"Gee, Pa, I didn't know that."

"What I'm trying to say is that I could change my will."

" 'Spect you could?"

"When my hands left Salt Creek with my race-horse I gave them strict orders to see that Deputy Sheriff Walt Grisham doesn't get back to Big Rock."

Coming to Kelsay Stuart now was a dawning of what this meant.

He said, "Isn't there another way . . ."

"No, son, as I've searched my soul for an answer. As I said, it's either them or us. 'Cause they hate us for what we have, son."

"You mean, Lily too? Pa, I . . ."

Dancy Stuart's hand came swinging in to strike his son across the bridge of his nose, and Kelsay fell onto his side. He moaned and came up holding his nose to stem the flow of blood, with shock spearing his eyes. Now he became fully aware of his father's madness; to save the family name murder must be committed. Maybe he'd known this before and once they'd left Salt Creek to come up here. That he was still clinging to the naïveté of youth.

"Listen to me now, Son," Dancy said with a show of patience he didn't feel. "There'll just be the tracker and those two deputy sheriffs and the girl. I've picked out a good spot to do it just downtrail a bit. Afterward we bring the bodies up there to put them amongst those dead outlaws. Just some lawmen and outlaws taking out one another."

Dancy Stuart turned his cup over to empty it out as his eyes hardened and he said, "Don't you dare let me down! You hear, Son!"

"The man's depraved as they come."

These words were spat out by Deputy Sheriff Walt Grisham sitting his horse as it labored up the narrow reaches of Lookout Pass. He was still a far piece from the summit. By rights he should be on his way home, but after all that had happened at Salt Creek, Grisham knew he had no other option. "Yup, Dancy Stuart's worse than the Kid, if that's possible."

The first part of it was when he'd packed Harv Black's body down to Salt Creek. Lucky for him it had been at night, or he would have been taken out by Dancy's renegade cowhands. It seemed even dogs hadn't set to braying to announce Grisham's arrival as he sighted in on the Lookout Saloon and the horses tied out front. Still, about a half block away there was enough light pouring out of the saloon so he could pick up on Dancy Stuart's brand on the near horse.

"Ain't in me to drink with cowards," muttered Grisham, and then he realized, when gazing further on, that the saloon was the only business place still open.

He wheeled in a couple of buildings short of the saloon to cut by a side wall and further on drew up by an old shed hemmed in by a rotting board fence. Tying up, he turned sorrowful eyes upon Harv Black's body wrapped in a yellow rain slicker. The sheriff would have to be buried here. Habit brought a hand to a shirt pocket before he remembered he was plumb out of the makings.

As he stood there silently deciding whether to go in to have a drink in the saloon, Walt Grisham turned over in his mind the tragedies suffered by this small cowtown. A name Bonner had mentioned came to mind: Hazel Enright. Though she was still alive, what she'd have to endure now was being called an unclean woman. All because she'd misjudged Kid LaDuke. So small this town, yet so full of busybodies, he reckoned. Is Big Rock any different?

"Got some want to mind my business there too," said Grisham as he patted the flank of his horse in stepping out through the litter toward the saloon. "Maybe I should bring Harv's body in there, so Dancy and them other cowards can get a good look. Dammit all."

At the moment Walt Grisham didn't know the reason for his actions as he cut around back of the saloon to come in by the side wall, instead of going in the back door. Here on the east wall there were three windows open to let in night air. At the first window he held up to sneak a look inside. And he was glad he did, as coming loud to him were the guarded words of Dancy Stuart, while through the screen on the window he could make out Dancy and cowhands Grisham knew, notably among them Frank Cafferty and Lem Dubay.

"Half the money'll be yours, Frank."

"A deal, Mr. Stuart. That okay with you, Lem?"

"All the way, Frank."

Lingering there, Deputy Grisham took in the pair of cowhands heading for the batwings. Grisham puzzled, "Money?" The only money the rancher had packed along had been exchanged for that racehorse. Must be it, him sending Cafferty and Dubay back up the pass.

Let them go, mused Grisham. His shoulder wouldn't quit aching and he felt light-headed. And whiskey would sure help take away the dryness in his mouth. Along with this came a well of anger as he found the side door and pushed into the saloon. He strode, spurs jangling, right to the bar, and deliberately ignoring Dancy Stuart gaping at him.

He plunked down a silver dollar, which brought the sad-eyed bartender reaching back for a bottle of whiskey. "Mister, you look in a bad way . . ."

"Felt worse. This town got a sawbones?"

"Just Granny Maddux; what you'd call a midwife."

"That'll do." He downed two quick drinks, the pain dulling away, and the whiskey settling warm and biting in his belly. Then he heard the tramp of boots, and without turning to look he knew it would be Dancy Stuart.

In a voice tight with anxiety the rancher said, "Where are the others—"

Grisham countered with, "Why in hell should you care, Mr. Stuart." Slowly he turned to lay contemptuous eyes upon the rancher. "Some are dead. But you, all you cared about was that worthless hunk of racehorse." He stared past the rancher at Kelsay Stuart hunkered low in a chair, the cowhands there unable to hold to his damning gaze.

To the bartender Grisham said, "Maybe you could direct me to this midwife . . ."

This was where Walt Grisham spent the night, in a back bedroom of the clapboard house owned by the midwife. But first he'd left Harv Black's body out in the woodshed and hobbled his bronc to let it graze under elm trees. Granny Maddux was a large woman with strands of untidy gray hair tied in a bun at the nape of her neck, and the deputy sheriff found her quite adept at treating gunshot wounds. He knew that during the night those waddies of Stuart's would be trying to find out where he'd be staying. But to the wounded deputy sheriff it didn't matter at all. As soon's his head hit the pillow he was sound asleep.

It was a different matter the next day, as Walt Grisham stole out early, just in time to catch a glimpse of Dancy Stuart and his son taking the western road out of Salt Creek. He was puzzling over this and keeping to the cover of a back alleyway when the rancher's hands headed the opposite way leading that prized racehorse.

211

"What is Dancy's game now?"

What Deputy Sheriff Grisham didn't know was that Dancy Stuart had ordered his men to set up an ambush. A ploy that went awry because Grisham knew that before he went anywhere his first duty was to have Sheriff Harvey Black laid to rest. And afterward, and despite his wound, he had no choice but to head up Lookout Pass again.

Now he reined up high in the colder recesses of the pass. With some effort he swung out of the saddle. He should have packed some grub along, but he shrugged the hunger pangs away. The sun came warming from the east out of a steely blue sky, building up his spirits some.

The way he figured it, Dancy Stuart would come across those dead bodies, and then press on. The money, maybe Dancy was after that, though Grisham felt that was only part of it.

There's his cowardice, the way Dancy took off up there. Something more than money involved here? Maybe some more killings.

Chapter Nineteen

More than anything Bonner Hudson hoped this was over. Last night he'd voiced to Jim Bob Benham his intentions of going on ahead, which he'd done long before daylight, keeping to the dark ribbon of stagecoach road.

Even when the sun rose east of the Bitterroots, Bonner found himself riding into shadow, where dew lay heavy on short grass and sagebrush. Though he could scarcely feel it, the road was beginning to creep up into the mouth of the canyon. And as he rode, at a lope, he realized it would be hard for someone lurking further up to sight in on him.

If indeed Dancy Stuart was holding up there, he'd have come in yesterday at the earliest. What impact would it have on Dancy coming onto those dead outlaws? Surely he wouldn't turn tail again, not after he'd tipped his hand by sending Cafferty and Dubay. Nope, this time Dancy had a lot more at stake than a racehorse.

Tucked into the folds of his sheepskin, Bonner

took stock of how many times he'd found himself in situations such as this, him tracking in behind some outlaws and them having the upper hand. Too many times, he reckoned. As there settled in his thoughts just how Angelica was taking this. Every day his wife would be looking down the road for a sign of him and Lily.

"Not fair to either of them," he lamented, "my hanging on as a tracker. Ranching, maybe . . ."

Another thought surfaced. "Jim Bob said I should run for sheriff. That would mean most everyone in the county turnin' my crank. This job's bad enough."

About a half mile into the canyon, he swung in to rest the bronc and to take a gander back at a valley floor dusted with morning sunlight. The others would be headed out now, but still a couple of hours behind. Subtly the darker fabric of night was lifting here under the high rocky prow of the mountain, of which Bonner was fully aware. Further up, the road hung on ledges, sheer cliff walls above which one misstep would take horse and rider over the edge. If anyone was lurking up there, he'd open up as it'd be like busting an eight ball off a billiard table.

"That eight ball just might be me."

For Rick McPherson the absence of Lily's father was greeted with an inward sigh of relief. But not so for Bonner's daughter when she was told about her father pulling out earlier to go on ahead.

"Doggonit, Jim Bob, what's going on—"

"Maybe nothing, young lady," he said, and swinging into the saddle.

"Jim Bob, it has something to do with those cowhands of Dancy Stuart's." Vaulting into the saddle, she reined after the deputy sheriff heading east along the narrow street. "So, what is it?"

"As I say, Lily, could be nothing. You know your pa, he's careful as they come. He went ahead, up into Lookout Pass; will be waitin' for us."

"Does it have something to do with that reward money you have in your saddlebags?"

"That is a tempting invitation, awright."

"Bonner told me all about Dancy pulling out up there. Is that it?"

"Could be, as your pa figures Dancy sent those cowhands of his'n back, that Cafferty, and Dubay. Bonner told me about Cafferty being a reformed high rider. Well, they're dead. But Dancy ain't; and he might be lurking up there."

"But . . . why?"

"Long's I've known that Dancy Stuart I've never figured him out. Don't figure either Dancy using his guns. But . . . your pa thinks otherwise."

"Then we'd better head after him," retorted Lily Hudson as she reined her bronc into a fast canter.

With a muttered oath Benham went after her, and when he came clattering alongside, he said firmly, "We tire our hosses out now, they won't last up there. Asides, Bonner ain't no fool as to let somethin' happen to him. We'll get there, gal, we'll get there."

215

They pressed on into the last reaches of the valley, and with Lily Hudson expecting to hear the rattling of gunfire, as by now they were about four miles from a scattering of chimney rock marking the entrance to the canyon. A band of sullen gray clouds covered part of the sun hanging over the Bitterroots.

Through all of this not once had she given thought to Kelsay Stuart, or the fact that he might be up there with his father. That Kelsay would go away to leave her to die had at first seemed shocking. As it had proved out Kelsay had no more bottom to him than one of her mother's pie tins. How long would it have been after they were married before he found someone more attractive? She'd heard of how Kelsay liked to hang around the saloons.

And to think I'd had notions of reforming him.
Back of her rode Rick McPherson, as his presence made Lily feel more comfortable about a lot of things. After all that had happened she still wasn't sure about her true feelings concerning this lanky deputy sheriff. It would take time, as she'd told Rick, to forget all that had happened in the last few days. A jocular musing came to mind of Mr. Rick McPherson making his intentions known to her father. Then she was jerking back her reins, as were the others, at the distant barking of a rifle.

A man could steel himself to being fired at, and

take other precautions, but it always jolted the nervous system to hear the reverberations of a high-powered rifle slapping against canyon walls.

In Bonner Hudson's case it was happening to him on an open stretch of high road with no place to go but back or pitch over the narrow ledge supporting this pebbly track. That single steel-jacketed bullet struck a couple of yards above his head to chip away stone fragments from the mountain wall bending over him.

"Get!"

Savagely he dug his spurs into the flanks of his bronc. It was Bonner's intention not to retreat but to go on, as higher up the trail widened out toward beckoning pines and huge boulders. Without thinking on it, he'd hunkered low over the saddle horn, and even as he made his dash for the haven above, his probing eyes were sweeping away up to the highest reaches of Lookout Pass.

Leaden slugs chipped the track behind their intended prey. The sun was a monstrous bedeviling ball striking into Bonner's eyes. Then he was almost there, veering off the track toward the screening trees, and with these fragmenting thoughts spilling out: *Only one rifle—an' the son-'bitch ain't all that good.*

He pulled in under a Douglas fir and reined up as under him the bronc was all atremble and fighting the reins. "Easy," Bonner murmured as it wheeled around, and as he swung down. Tying the reins to a stout branch, he worked upslope amid the trees to where he had a clear view of everything above. He could pretty well picture the ambusher to one side of the track close and bellied down on flat rocks. From where he stood under the trees the track curled one way and then another toward the summit, which was more open than the eastern side, where there were all those rocks.

"Still plenty of open places to pass along," Bonner considered; he would be like a black speck on a sheet of white paper. But a plan was unfolding; he had a feeling that it wasn't just a single rifleman up there.

Along with this came a fretting worry, but he chased this away—he knew Jim Bob wouldn't endanger the others by doing anything rash. Now he trudged back to his horse. From his saddlebag he removed his hunting knife, and he went in search of some branches. After he'd secured some branches that would suit his purposes, he cut away the leaves and set about tying them together with short pieces of rope he cut from his riata. Out of his saddlebags came a spare shirt, which he fitted over the tied branches. Removing his Stetson, he wedged it on next, then he used more rope to fasten what he'd made to his saddle.

"There. Skinnier'n me, but it might work."

Shucking out of his boots, he found the pair of moccasins he always packed along and put them on. As he did, he had to smile at the bronc twisting its head around to take a gander at the thing roped to the saddle. Then Bonner swung up behind what appeared to be another person sharing the saddle. He brought the bronc on at a walk under the trees until the flat plateau closed in on the track curling upward. He reached down to un- sheathe his rifle, and held there for a moment, hoping wistfully that those few low clouds to the east might come in over the sun.

Finally he muttered, "Well, you ready, hoss?"

The curses of Dancy Stuart kept ringing out to his son, who cowered just across the track in a jumble of rocks. "Dammit, Kelsay, we coulda taken him out if you'd opened up. Dammit, boy, he made it to them trees."

The rancher swung up an angry hand to tug his hat back, as he turned glaring eyes from his son back to the canyon opening up below him. It was less than a half mile to where he'd first spotted Bonner Hudson. He should have waited until the tracker got in closer, but as he considered himself something of a marksman, he felt he couldn't miss. But he had, and he explained it away by tell- ing himself it was damned hard judging distances when firing downslope. He felt confident, though, that he had the tracker boxed in, and now Dancy Stuart frowned as questions flickered in his eyes.

"Seems strange it's only Bonner. What happened to Cafferty, Dubay? And Bonner's girl . . . the others, damn, I don't like this." He cried out now, "Kelsay, keep your eyes peeled." He wormed around to reach out for his canteen.

Across the trail the fears of Kelsay Stuart were

evident in the way his hands were trembling. If he could leave he would, for he'd never seen his father worked up like this before, just itching to kill someone. Which only brought home to Kelsay that he didn't really know Dancy Stuart. It wasn't all that warm as yet, but he was sweating, chiefly out of his fears about killing someone and his fear of his father.

It took him a moment to realize that a horseman was filling the track below as he fumbled with his rifle while yelling, "Pa, he's there!"

"Then open up!" came Dancy Stuart's raging cry, and with Dancy grabbing his own weapon and sighting it in on the track. Grimly he heard his son's rifle bark, then he was opening up on the tracker and at the same time unsure about what he was seeing. "Damn!" His curse was for the horseman vanishing just for a moment from his eye wedged in close to his rifle sight. Then the tracker reappeared still in the saddle and coming up the track.

Just before this, Bonner had reined up hard behind the scant cover of some boulders, and quickly he'd swung down to tie the reins to the saddle horn. Quickly too he'd lifted up the back of the saddle to slip a couple of small pine cones under the wide expanse of cherry-leather saddle. Then he'd slammed his fist down hard on the saddle to have the horse bolt up the trail and into the open again.

Now Bonner Hudson kept to rocky cover and the scattering of pines as he worked up the canyon, while further up Dancy Stuart blasted away at the oncoming horse and that awkward-looking rider sitting squared up in the saddle. The rancher rose up, moved further along the track, and fired away, unaware that higher up on the mountain the shattering gunfire had caused a slight ripple of movement. First it was some small pebbles being dislodged by the shock waves of sound, and come down to dislodge larger stones; then the barest of rockslides started, to come down a chute and strike into larger rocks. Below the pathway of falling rocks moved Dancy Stuart.

A triumphant glare gaped his eyes open further as the bronc took a hit in the chest and broke stride. And when it did, it suddenly came to Dancy Stuart that it wasn't the tracker in the saddle but something else, while further up from him his son picked up on the faint rumble of sound coming from above.

Glancing upward, Kelsay Stuart saw the dust made by the falling rockslide, and he froze, unable to cry out or rise. But even now it was too late; the rocks were a vengeful mass of weight sweeping down toward the track. Just for a second Dancy Stuart was aware of the peril, then the rancher was gone, as was part of the track. The grinding roar of the rockslide continued on down into the deepest recesses of the canyon.

Some time later Bonner Hudson appeared to work his way cautiously around the gaping tear in the trail. He'd been lifting his rifle to bear it in on Dancy Stuart, and even then he was hesitant about firing. Bonner hadn't been primed to kill; he wanted to take Dancy alive. He wanted to bring Dancy back to answer for all of this.

Reckon he angered the mountain gods.

Movement above caught his eye, and he crouched to bring up his rifle, and again he held from firing. Coming down in a shambling walk was Dancy's son, not holding any weapon. He stopped just short of Bonner and looked about blindly, his eyes stung with tears. Sobbingly he muttered, "He was . . . he wanted to kill . . ."

"He's gone, Son . . ."

Just like that it was over, and Bonner felt drained of emotion. He didn't speak or try to stop Kelsay Stuart as the young man swung away. For Kelsay would have to live with his father's shame. The regret Bonner felt now was for the dead bronc, as in turning he saw, still some distance out, the others coming up the pass. He unleathered his six-gun and triggered it three times.

Two days later they were coming into Camas Prairie and glimpsing the Flathead Valley again when a lone horseman appeared, and Bonner Hudson swung out ahead of the others. All he could do when he reached his wife Angelica was to grasp her outstretched hand and murmur quietly, "I brought our daughter back."

"I see that. I couldn't wait there any longer."

"Tracking, I'm done with it."

"Life without it could be different . . ."

"Life without you or Lily is a lonely thought. Well, there's our cabin to rebuild. One thing, it

222

won't have to be as large. As I believe our daughter has weddin' plans. But not to Kelsay. Come on, I'll explain it best I can on the way home."